Brennan
207

Brennan
207

I Don't Belong Here

SOFIA MAZLOUM

Copyright © 2014 Sofia Mazloum.

All rights reserved. No part of this book may be used or reproduced by any means, graphic, electronic, or mechanical, including photocopying, recording, taping or by any information storage retrieval system without the written permission of the publisher except in the case of brief quotations embodied in critical articles and reviews.

Balboa Press books may be ordered through booksellers or by contacting:

Balboa Press
A Division of Hay House
1663 Liberty Drive
Bloomington, IN 47403
www.balboapress.com.au
1 (877) 407-4847

Because of the dynamic nature of the Internet, any web addresses or links contained in this book may have changed since publication and may no longer be valid. The views expressed in this work are solely those of the author and do not necessarily reflect the views of the publisher, and the publisher hereby disclaims any responsibility for them.

This is a work of fiction. All of the characters, names, incidents, organizations, and dialogue in this novel are either the products of the author's imagination or are used fictitiously.

Any people depicted in stock imagery provided by Thinkstock are models, and such images are being used for illustrative purposes only. Certain stock imagery © Thinkstock.

Printed in the United States of America.

ISBN: 978-1-4525-2531-0 (sc)
ISBN: 978-1-4525-2532-7 (e)

Balboa Press rev. date: 09/02/2014

Thank you to my family and friends for all your support and particularly to my cousin Sana and my brother Hadi for being on this journey with me from the beginning. Thank you as always to my students for your inspiration.

CHAPTER 1

I STEPPED OFF THE TRAIN and headed home. Before I reached for my front door, I took a deep breath. I stepped inside, expecting the worst, but hoping he was in a good mood.

"Where have you been, young lady?" my father asked in Arabic, not looking at me as his eyes were transfixed on the television. So much for wishful thinking!

"At Melbourne Uni, Dad, for the Open Day," I replied, annoyed at the fact that he always talked to me in Arabic. It was his way of making sure I never forgot my first language.

His eyes tore themselves away from the Al Jazeera news and bore a hole through my soul. "Do not dare take that patronising tone of voice with me! I know where you were, but why are you an hour late?"

"It ran a bit later than expected," I managed to finally mutter, lowering my eyes and praying my face did not look as flushed as it felt. *Seriously, my tone was not patronising, you freaking arrogant Lebo!*

"Well, we ate without you. Your mother has left something in the oven for you. I should punish you for letting your brother know you were running late and not us. Why is it easier for you kids to punch so many keys and send a … a text message, is it?" I nodded, but I really just wanted to roll my eyes at his terrible Arab accent. I wouldn't dare, though.

"Easier than just calling home and saying you are running late?" he continued. "I do not understand the logic behind your actions!" I remained silent and wondered how long the lecture would last.

"You are apparently a smart girl, Tamara, yet you never have anything intelligent to say," he paused, waiting for me to make some kind of response. I didn't.

"Get out of my sight!" he ordered after I continued to stare intently at the rug under my feet.

"OK …" I mumbled inaudibly, bolting out of the living room before he threw something at me. But if he dared, I would throw something back. Now that would make me feel warm and fuzzy inside, but I didn't have the courage. I had copped my fair share of verbal and physical abuse. Thank God we had overcome that stage. My mother always used to repeat this Arabic saying whenever my father hit me: "Whoever hits you loves you." How fucked up is that! Punishing a child through physical abuse is a way of showing that you care for their well-being? What bullshit! I would never forget the last time he hit me. I was twelve years old. I had stated that I didn't want to go home but would rather hang out at the restaurant a while longer. Dad lost it and embarrassed me in front of my aunt by welting my arms with his belt. That was when this voice inside my head became louder and stronger. If only I were strong enough to listen to that stronger side of myself all the time, but I lacked that confidence.

"Hi, Mum," I said as I walked into the kitchen.

"Hi, Tamara. How was it?" she asked while placing a ridiculously overflowing plate of fatoush, a Lebanese bread salad, in front of me.

"Yeah, it was good. Informative," I answered, always glad that she practiced her English with me.

"Well, you clean your room before study because I cleaned too much already today," she stated, opening the dishwasher.

"Alright, Mum. Relax, I will."

"Don't speak like that to me, Tamara. I am not one of your friends!"

"OK, sorry," I replied as she began to rinse the dishes.

"Tamara, I don't like to be noisy, but do you do drugs with your friends?"

"Mum, it's nosy, not noisy. And as if I would ever! God knows what Hitler incarnate would do to me if I ever did!" I stated, flinging my fork down on my plate.

"Don't call your father that, Tamara. You know he is only strict because he loves you."

"Yeah, whatevs. Why are you asking if I'm doing drugs, Mum?" I should ask her about the multitude of prescriptions in her bathroom.

"Because you speak rudely now. There's no respect anymore from you kids!"

"Puh-lease, Mum! Your son talks to you like you are nothing! Don't associate me with the way he is because I never speak to you disrespectfully. I can't believe you really just accused me of taking drugs!" I pushed my plate away and headed upstairs to my room. I was so sick of her taking out her anger on me. What was I, everyone's freaking punching bag?

I sat on my bed and closed my eyes. This was my sanctuary, the one place where anything could happen. My fantasies could take me anywhere I wanted to be. I could live life through my wild imagination.

"Hey, Sis!"

My eyes instantly opened, and I glared at my brother. "How many times do I have to tell you to fucking knock?" I threw my pillow at him, which he skilfully caught.

"Duh! You actually think the best goalie in the world couldn't catch that?" he stated, dancing on the spot.

"Piss off."

"Ah … no! You owe me big time, bro," he replied, slumping down on my bed.

"Don't freaking call me bro! Just get out!"

"What's up your ass?" He always said *ass* with an American accent, and it would make me wish more than anything that I had anyone, anyone at all, other than him as my brother.

"And you wonder why I don't like being seen with you in public?" I stated sarcastically.

"What do you mean?" he whined childishly as I gave him what I called my indifferent stare. For a fifteen year old he acted more like he was two. "Anyway, I'm gonna see Amelia but tell Dad you organised for one of your friends to tutor me. Let's say Sarah. Yeah, Sarah. Cause she likes earning money."

"Whatever, she's not really my friend." I mumbled as I turned away from him and buried my face in my pillow. As I heard the door shut behind him, I dreamt of the day when I would be free of this dysfunctional family, free of my culture, and free of my tyrannical father. That day would take many years of study and hard work to make possible, but I knew that it would eventually happen (or at least I held onto the hope that it simply had to). I was the catalyst for that much-needed change. I really needed to stop talking to myself!

My thoughts returned to the hot student I saw at Melbourne Uni with his gorgeous sea-green eyes. I wished I could be *that* girl, the one who attracted boys like a magnet. But I wasn't! No one ever approached me. Once when I was talking to my cousin's friend, I blushed and stuttered so much that *he* began turning red. I was mortified when he mumbled something and tore off like the devil was chasing him. My shyness repelled guys. Damn, I had been sheltered so much. Seriously, if I became promiscuous overnight, it would be due to my parents never allowing me to experience anything.

★ ★ ★

The following Saturday started like every other before it: helping Mum clean the house while she spent hours in the kitchen. I managed to spend a few hours on my English essay, much to my mother's dismay. She likes to have company while she cooks. But I was still annoyed at her from the other day. One thing I have always vowed was to never become a housewife whose only purpose in life was to slave away for her husband and kids. Sure, I was being slightly harsh here, but that is the only life my mother had ever known. She married my dad at the age of eighteen, three months after they met, convinced that he was the one! Yeah, right! I heard her tell my Auntie Lydia once that she had naively tried to "lose" my brother by slamming her fists into her stomach. I assumed that she didn't want him because it would have been easier to run away with just one kid. She believed that I had no awareness of her unhappiness, and she did hide it well by blaming her bad moods on our behaviour. On rare occasions, she would tell me stories about her life before she got married and how she was the most beautiful of all her sisters. Other stories, too, about how she was so wild that her father would yell and punish her every day, but she would still sneak out to do what she wanted. I envied her strength, particularly her defiance against her father, and wished she had passed that down to me.

My cousin Sara texted me at six and asked if I wanted to go to the movies. I replied that there was no way I would be allowed. I then heard our house phone ring, and after a few minutes, my dad called my name.

"Tamara," he began as I walked into the living room. "Your aunt just called and asked if you would like to go watch a movie with Sara tonight."

"It would be a great break from all this study, Dad," I replied, lowering my eyes.

"OK then. She will be here in half an hour. Go get changed out of those terrible sporty clothes." I looked at him with bewilderment and figured that my auntie must be a miracle worker. I changed into my favourite jeans, a warm top, and casual boots. Smiling happily, I bolted down the stairs. Before I walked out the door, Dad pulled me aside, almost yanking my wrist off my arm.

"If I hear that you did anything reckless or stupid tonight, you will never be allowed out with Sara again. Understand?"

"Yes, Dad." I tried not to let my abhorrence of him seep out of my eyes.

"Look at me when I'm talking to you." I met his eyes as my hands quivered slightly. "You be the good girl I raised, and do not disappoint me, Tamara. You will be the only one who suffers the consequences of your bad decisions."

"Yes, Dad," I replied as I turned very slowly and walked out of the house. *You weak, sorry excuse for a father! Hope you die a miserable and slow death one day.*

"*Khalto*, Auntie. How did you convince him to let me go?" I asked as I fastened my seatbelt.

"*Habibi,* honey. You know I would do anything to get you out of that prison," my aunt informed me as she leaned over and gave me a peck on the cheek. She promised my dad she would pick us up the minute the movie ended. I was surprised he was so OK with this arrangement considering he didn't think highly of my aunt since her divorce. I shrugged and whispered in Sara's ear, asking whether Shadi was meeting us.

"Like tots! You don't have to whisper. Mum knows Shadi's my boyfriend."

"What?!" I finally managed to squeak after a long moment of shock.

"Shadi is a very sweet boy, and I trust Sara. If only your dad would do the same. Then he would never have to worry about you doing something crazy and rebellious one day. Tamara, I wouldn't blame you if you did."

"Why can't all mums be as cool as you, *khalto*?"

"Don't blame your mother. She has it harder than you can ever imagine."

"Don't worry; I know!" She looked at me long and hard through the rear view mirror.

"Anyway, have fun, girls. Love you and be good," she said as she gave us both a kiss on the cheek.

"*Yalla*, hurry up. He's probably waiting already. He has this weird thing about punctuality. Oh, and by the way, he brought his best mate along, Adrian. He's single." She squealed a little too loud for my liking.

"Shhh! Do you want the whole world to hear you? Why would you do that, Sara? You know I can't hook up with anyone, like, ever! Not until I'm over thirty or something. Dad would murder me first! You know he would never allow me to get married so young like he and mum did."

"Who says he needs to know or will ever find out? And why are you talking about marriage? You are such a tripper!" she whispered and gave me her perfect cheeky smile. I trudged along, terrified of meeting Adrian or someone seeing us and informing my father. The consequences would be terrifying.

CHAPTER 2

"Hey," Adrian said, holding out his hand.

"Hi," I managed to mutter back as I placed my palm in his. He smiled, and I knew I was smiling back my nervous grin that made me look whacked. I checked the movie ticket for our cinema number as an excuse to avoid eye contact with Adrian. Shadi cleared his throat and suggested we head into the theatre. I looked at Adrian out of the corner of my eye and admired his boyish looks. He looked so Mediterranean with his light blue eyes and jet black hair. He also had a typical Italian nose, but with that olive skin, he was pretty hot. He wasn't the type of guy I would normally go for, like the gorgeous one I had noticed at Melbourne Uni, but he was still really good-looking. As I sat down and started munching away at the popcorn, I noticed Adrian smirking at me.

"What?" I asked, raising my eyebrows.

"It's good to see you didn't try to find the fat and carb content on the packet before you dug in."

"Popcorn is my addiction; it's what allows me to keep going after studying for five hours straight," I said with a shrug.

"Well, I like a girl who likes to eat as much as me." He dug his hand in and took a big handful of popcorn. He must work out because he sure looked good for someone who likes to eat. I turned to my left and noticed that Sara and Shadi were already at it, making out like they hadn't seen each other in years. I studied them for a bit too long and turned back towards the screen. I was yet to experience my first proper French kiss. I know, I know! How sad, right? A sixteen-year-old who has only ever been pecked on the lips.

"So you like it so far?"

"What?" I muttered turning towards him to find his face very close to mine.

"The movie?"

"Yeah, not bad … typical romantic comedy. Too predictable and bet ya fifty bucks that it will end with a marriage or sex scene." I bit my lip and cursed myself silently. *Why, oh why did you say that?* He probably thinks that I'm conceited. I usually watch movies alone, on DVD, and I always talk to myself as I analyse them, hoping that one day I could write a much better script.

"Yeah, you're right. They do always end the same," he stated casually.

"How many chick flicks have you watched?"

"Heaps! My sister always makes me sit through them so she can get a guy's perspective," he informed me as he rolled his eyes. I laughed with relief.

"I didn't mean to sound so pretentious before," I said as I lowered my eyes.

"It's OK," he took my hand and held it gently. "I like a girl who speaks her mind."

My heart started beating erratically. His hand was so warm and smoother than I had imagined. I looked into his blue eyes and found so much warmth there. How was it that he was so confident and comfortable while I was sitting here scared shitless? I felt a stabbing pain in my side and turned to find Sara grinning at me as she looked from my face to my hand. I rolled my eyes at her and turned back towards Adrian, who was back to watching the movie. A kissing scene soon came on, and I took my hand out of his and rummaged through my handbag. I checked my phone and put it away just as quickly. Coward!

As soon as my hand was free again, he grabbed it and placed it in his. He was staring at me with such deep concentration that it caused the lines on his forehead to appear. I looked into his eyes once again and forced myself not to turn away as his face moved closer and closer towards mine. I closed my eyes and prayed I wouldn't make a complete fool of myself. As we moved towards one another, our mouths met and our teeth clattered against each other. I pulled away and mumbled a mortified apology. He placed his fingers under my chin and forced my eyes to meet his. He leaned over once again, and I was annoyed at myself for not knowing what to do despite having studied so many French kissing scenes in movies. He increased the pressure of his lips, and I opened mine to kiss him back. His tongue soon found mine, and as our breathing quickened, I wondered what I should do with my hands. His hands moved to my back as he awkwardly pushed my body closer to his. I felt like I was being consumed by a warm bubble as my body tingled all over. When the tingling subsided, I stroked Adrian's face and ran my other hand through his curly hair. The rest of the movie was watched in snippets because Adrian would not stop kissing me.

As we walked out, I gave him my number and a quick kiss. Nothing else mattered at that moment. I didn't care if someone had seen me kiss him or if my aunt was watching. I only knew that this was the first boy I had ever really kissed and that meant something. *Yeah, it meant that he would be the first boy you screw!* Ahhh! How could I think such things!

I could feel my face beaming as I said hi to my aunt. He texted me straight away and said that he couldn't wait to see me again. I was flying on a magic carpet, and there was nothing that could bring me down. Experience, however, has taught me that when I am on a high, I always come crashing down. Who knew how long this euphoria would last?

★ ★ ★

That night, I had a dream that Adrian was having dinner at my place. My father was beaming at him and me with so much pride and joy. I sighed sadly when I woke up and realised that that day would probably only happen when I was thirty, and instead of Adrian, an arrogant Lebo would be sitting beside me. I placed my hand on my lips and brought back the warm memories of his kiss. I still felt tingly all over, and I couldn't stop smiling to myself.

I opened the door to the living room, and as my eyes met those of my father, I instantly felt that something was terribly wrong.

"Sit down!" I nervously took a seat and almost landed on the floor.

"What did you watch last night? Who were you with?"

"Um, we watched a romantic comedy, and I was with Sara."

"So just you and your cousin went to the movies?"

"Yes, Dad," I gulped as my face turned crimson red. God, I was such a bad liar!

"How do you feel about lying to your father?"

"What … what do you mean, Dad? I've never lied to you." The shaking in my voice betrayed me.

"Not only do you dishonour your father, but you also look him right in the eyes and lie to his face! Your cousin Rami saw exactly who you were with and what you were doing last night. And you will never disgrace this family like that again. Do you hear me? How could you be such a …?" I knew he was going to say slut but stopped himself in time.

"Look at me when I am talking to you! You betrayed my trust and your aunt's. I cannot believe you would be stupid enough to think that you are old enough to have a boyfriend," he stated as the muscles in his neck started to bulge out.

"Dad, he's not my boyfriend!" Good one.

"Not your boyfriend? You are acting like you were raised on the streets. No self-respect! Who is this boy, anyway?"

"His name is Adrian. Adrian Fontana. I am sixteen years old, Dad. I think I am more than old enough to have a boyfriend!" You go, girl!

"Do not speak to me like that, young lady! You are grounded for the rest of the year," he boomed as he slammed his fist on the table.

"But …" He held up his hand, and I instantly closed my mouth. I knew that look in his eyes, and pushing him any further would cause dire consequences. *Stop being such a coward,* I thought. I looked at my brother who was standing in the doorway and wondered what kind of punishment he would have received if he was caught kissing Amelia, probably a playful punch on the shoulder and a few words of encouragement. I looked over at my mother, but she wouldn't look me in the eyes. *She is a coward, too. You take after her!* I walked to my room at a snail's pace and kept my ears open for the sound of my brother's footsteps. I turned around and raised my middle finger in his direction. *Thanks for the warning, shithead!*

"What the? What were ya thinking, midget?"

"CBF, Charlie!" I replied as I turned away from him.

"How could you be so stupid?"

"Piss off!" I slammed the door in his face and collapsed with my back against the door. All this fuss over a freaking kiss! I wondered what he would have done if I had slept with the guy—most probably kicked me out with only the clothes on my back. I was living in a free country! Why could I not live a normal teenage life? All the Anglo girls I knew at school lived a normal life without all this drama. The tears would not stop flowing as I lamented my cursed life and thought about how I was never going to see Adrian again. I wanted the freedom to live some kind of a life, but that was impossible while I was living under this roof and impossible while I was part of this family that held onto stupid Middle Eastern rules!

CHAPTER 3

Every Monday morning, we would drive our teachers crazy by chatting nonstop about our weekends. I stood at my locker, patiently listening to my best friend, Fiona, talk about her never-ending family feuds. Fiona came from a strict Italian family, and her father was just as dictating as mine. Mariam, our other best friend, joined the conversation and added to it with a recap of her crazy mother's latest rant. Lunch time came, and we sat in our miserable circle feeling sorry for ourselves.

"Fi, how much do you like this guy?" I asked wondering how long this particular love interest of hers would last.

"I think I might love him!" she replied with a dramatic sigh.

"But you barely know him. You haven't spoken more than two sentences to him, and he hasn't even held your hand." Mariam was always the voice of reason; we called her the bitch of the group.

"But he couldn't keep his eyes off my tits, and that's proof enough for me that he wants me." Fiona giggled her little laugh. She was the bimbo (obviously), and I, much to my dismay, was labelled the doormat.

"Fi, what makes Tony so special compared to all the other guys you have met?" Mariam asked.

"Cause I have met so many!" she stated, rolling her eyes. "I just like him OK. Tam, hun, tell your dad to go to hell, and see Adrian again."

"You first, and then I'll follow your lead." We stared each other down and then burst out laughing.

"Hey, at least your mother doesn't go see the priest every time something unorthodox happens in her house." We laughed even louder, and Mariam joined us. We have been the three stooges since year seven. When all the other girls branched out in their friendship groups, we were the remaining three girls. Since then, nothing could separate us.

"Tam, you skimmed over the recap of your first kiss, and I want to know all the gory details."

"There isn't much to tell, Mi Mi."

"Don't call me that. You know how much I hate it when Mum does. And come on, you are the only one that has been kissed. Please give us some advice for when we finally get the chance, if we ever do! All I wish is for Karim to notice me," Mariam stated, sighing.

"If I were you, I would just go up to him and talk to him at church. No one will notice." She rolled her eyes at me, and I shrugged. "Look, girls: If it weren't for my cousin, I would never have hooked up with Adrian. I think all you two need is a push in the right direction."

"And I bet you wanna do the honours!"

"Sure, Mi Mi. Why not?" I replied as I raised my eyebrows.

"You aren't getting out of this! What was it like?"

"Honestly, the whole time I was scared shitless that someone would see us. I wish I could have Sara's life. She has her mother's support, and she can see Shadi whenever she wants." I sighed and continued, "not only was I worried about someone seeing us, but I was also terrified about the kiss itself. It's not like in the movies; it's not in the least bit perfect! It was like my skin had pins and needles. At first, our teeth clattered, which was *so* embarrassing, but then as we kissed some more, it turned to French."

"Ohhh," they both cooed.

"Anyway, once we both felt more comfortable, we couldn't keep our hands off each other. He was still a perfect gentleman, but touching lips wasn't enough, hands had to touch skin to feel even closer … you know … " You could tell from the looks on their faces that they clearly did not know.

"Trust me, when you experience your first kiss, it will be really weird and awkward, but with practice, you will get better at it.'

"You're so lucky, Tam," Fiona muttered with dreamy eyes.

"Yeah … very …" I sighed and played with the edge of my school dress. *Stop feeling sorry for yourself.*

"Hey, did you hear about Rania?" Mariam asked, pointing over to the lone figure near the basketball courts.

"What about her?"

"Tam, I can't believe you don't know. You're Lebo. You should know everything about other Lebos. You all gossip like crazy!"

"Right! Like I am *so* interested in the Lebanese community."

"Anyway, she's pregnant, and her parents kicked her out. She is staying at her aunt and uncle's. She's going to have an abortion."

"Oh my God! That's epic, poor girl," Fi exclaimed, looking over at Rania with a sympathetic smile.

"So why won't she keep it?" I asked.

"Because her dad gave her an ultimatum: an abortion or he will kill her, more likely disown her," Mariam answered rolling her eyes.

"Shit! Who's the father?" Fiona asked.

"This Lebo Muslim, Wissam, which her parents would never approve of! They've been going out for two years. He wants to marry her and support them both, but his parents are giving him an earful, too. Rania decided on the abortion and then broke up with him. He has brought as much shame on his family as she has," Mariam said that last line with her dad's Arab accent, and we all laughed.

"You know, it would be the perfect way to get out."

"Huh?" Fi replied putting away her compact mirror.

"I said, Miss Vain that getting pregnant would be the perfect way of getting out of our prisons and I bet you think this song is about you."

"Haha! But seriously, Tam. You wouldn't get yourself pregnant just so you can get disowned? And you said you wanted to wait," Mariam stated.

"Not until marriage; that's just stupid! But yeah, I do wanna wait for that someone special and make it real romantic. But then again if it happens, it happens," I replied with a mischievous smile.

"You're so full of shit!" Fiona stated.

"At least I am not obsessed with my looks, bimbo!"

"Hey! Well how … how am I meant to answer back to that?" We all laughed again.

"Tam, stop thinking stupid things and think about your future. How would you become a psychologist and a writer if you had a baby to look after?"

"Good point, Mariam. Maybe I can study from home and do an online course."

"Just shut up; I've heard enough. You think you're the most rebellious of us all, but any bet you will be the last to lose your virginity."

"Nah, you will forever be the Virgin Mary, Mi Mi. Your Egyptian psycho religion demands it of you!" She threw her jumper at my face, and Fi and I laughed at her. She tried to hide her smile as she got up to go to class.

"Hurry up. We're gonna be late for religion, and you know how much Mr Arnold hates that. But then again, staying in after school will give us more time in his heavenly presence," Mariam cried out, with as much passion as one of Shakespeare's heroines. We laughed all the way to class and received detention not for being late but for laughing so much every time Mariam made faces at Mr Arnold.

As Miss Mitchell saw us leaving the detention room, I noticed her surprised expression. She always valued our good behaviour as we were the nerdiest girls in our year level. I was sure Miss Mitchell would be even more surprised when she found out Mariam was the instigator of our punishment. Mariam was the smartest girl in year ten, and everyone said she would most definitely get Dux in year twelve. I turned to my left and noticed Rania walking out of the main office. She strolled past us and gave me a dirty look. As I turned towards Fiona and Mariam, I heard her say "So the little angel has gotten into trouble: About fucking time!" I spun around to confront her, but she had already walked into our year ten building. What was her freaking problem?

As I waved goodbye to my besties, I found Adrian waiting for me outside the school gates. I froze and just stared at him. He looked gorgeous standing there, and he somehow managed to look cool and decent in his school uniform. I stepped forward and hesitated. *Hurry up, gutless!* I looked around and walked towards him.

"What are you doing here?" I whispered, tugging him behind a wall so that my teachers wouldn't see us.

"I hate communicating through texts, and you can't talk to me at home because of your dad, so I came to see you in person," he said while trying to lean over to kiss me.

"Are you crazy?" I slipped under his arms and quickly walked away from school. He followed, and as soon as we were out of sight, I gave him a warm hug.

"Do you know how many girls here are Lebos? The Lebanese community plays Chinese whispers, and by the time it gets back to my dad, I'll be the girl who was seen walking out of a hotel with you instead of school." He didn't reply but looked deep into my eyes and ran his fingers through my hair.

"Your hair is so silky," he said, and I melted. He leaned over, and I threw my arms around him and welcomed his lips with my own. I must admit he was a damn good kisser. We walked to the park hand in hand and sat down on a secluded bench. I leaned my head on his shoulder and chipped away at the wooden table in front of us with my nails.

"This is such a big risk, Adrian. Shit! Hang on!" I called Mum and told her I was going to be a bit late as I was getting some books from the library. "Lies and more lies. That's what my life revolves around," I muttered, turning my face towards his broad chest. He placed his fingers under my chin and forced my eyes to meet his. He kissed me lightly on the nose and then moved his lips to mine. Our breathing quickened as our kisses became more passionate. I giggled when his tongue licked at my earlobe and squealed when he bit it.

"I can't see you again, Adrian. It's just too risky." I thought, *No you won't be stupid enough to let this one go! Focus on him, Tam!*

"Whatever … who cares?"

"You will if my father catches us. Trust me." I pushed him away. "If you want … I mean … if you like me enough … I mean …" I sighed with exasperation and started again, "We just have to wait."

"For what?"

I sighed once again, "Until I'm eighteen … I don't know … that's when hopefully I'll make money from my writing and be able to move out." I realised how ridiculous I sounded, and I shook my head in distress.

"You write?"

"Yep. In my stories, I can be anyone." He ran his fingers through my hair again and leaned forward to kiss me.

"No, I mean it, Age," I said as I turned my face away and stood up. "Just say goodbye and promise you won't text or try to see me again."

"I can't do that!" He shrugged and began to walk away.

"Adrian!" I yelled out while stamping my foot. *Oh puh-lease! Stop acting like such a child and just jump on him already. Go somewhere a bit more private! Shhh!*

"You looked like you were ten just then!" he called out, laughing.

"So not funny. Promise me!"

"I promise you, Tamara Khoury, that I will not try to not see you again." It took me a few moments to make sense of his words, and by that time, he had already left the park.

"Boys are so infuriating," I mumbled under my breath as I headed home.

CHAPTER 4

Friday finally arrived, and I was allowed out of my cell since Dad thought I had a debating meeting. For every previous meeting, I asked for money to buy dinner but didn't eat so that I could save that money for an emergency. Maybe for the day when I would need a motel because I could no longer stand living under his roof. Debating had finished last week, but thankfully, Dad didn't know that. I went down to Melbourne Uni, I didn't know where else to go as Sara was probably on a date with Shadi since she hadn't texted me to come over. I walked into the Baillieu Library and straight up to the fiction section. I walked up and down the aisles, running my fingers across the spines of the novels, and started daydreaming of the day when I would be here researching for an essay. After much contemplation, I decided on Austen and found *Pride and Prejudice*. Although I had read it countless times, it was one of those novels I could pick up and skim through to my favourite parts. On my way home, I decided to go past the cafe in front of the law building to grab a chai latte. As I waited in line to order, a guy walked over and stood next to me. I glanced at him and realised he was *the* guy, the one I had noticed from the open day. I started fidgeting. I tried to act cool, but he was just so hot and made me so nervous that I dropped my change right at his feet.

"Sorry," I mumbled, too mortified to meet his eyes.

"No worries," he replied as he bent down to help me pick the coins up. I glanced up at him and smiled weakly. *God! I am such an embarrassment!* As we were both waiting for our drinks, I tried my hardest to stop looking at him. My eyes had a mind of their own, though. When his gorgeous green eyes met mine, I turned away quickly and blushed uncontrollably. Our drinks were ready at the same time, and my hand brushed his as I reached up to grab my chai. It was as if an electric current had passed from his hand to mine and I finally admitted to myself that I was crazy.

"Hey, you dropped this." I turned around and met his eyes. I glanced down at the two sachets of sugar and the small plastic spoon, which must have fallen off the lid in my hurried attempt to get away from him.

"Thanks," I muttered.

"No worries," he replied with a perfect smile.

"And thanks for helping with my change, too."

"Anytime," he replied. He paused and continued, "Do you go here?"

"Sorry?"

"Are you studying law?"

"Oh. Um, nah. I hope to study here next year, though. I'm still in year twelve!" *What are you doing?*

"Cool. I think I saw you here at the open day."

"Yeah, I came to that. Do you study here?" Oh. My. God. He remembered me! Ahhh! *Do not freak out now. This guy is gorgeous. If you scare him off and don't hook up with him, I will never let you live it down! Oh God! When was I going to stop talking to myself like I am talking to another person? I was sure it was not mentally healthy!*

"Yeah, I do law/commerce."

"Awesome, must be all brain-consuming." *What does that mean? What is wrong with me?*

"No kidding. So what are you doing here tonight?"

"Um ... just checked some books out at the library, but they weren't that helpful."

"Cool. Hey, if you're not busy next Friday, I'm having a BBQ and a few drinks at my place. Swing past if you like," he asked as nonchalantly as one would comment about the weather.

"Thanks, maybe," was all I could reply. *Good one!*

"Well I live on campus, Queens College, room seventeen. The party starts at seven," he informed me with a shrug of his shoulders.

"OK, thanks. I'll try to make it," I replied as I tried to remember his room number while giving him a saucy smile.

"Cool. See ya later. Oh, by the way, my name is James."

"Ah, I'm, mine is Tamara." *Oh God!*

"See ya maybe Friday," he smiled warmly and strolled away as I stood there in utter shock.

★ ★ ★

As I stared at my computer screen at seven in the evening the next night and lamented my cursed life *again*, our doorbell rang. A few minutes later, Sara rushed into my room.

"Wow, cuz! Homework on a Saturday night? Thrilling!"

"I'm actually writing as I'm hoping to enter this competition."

"Bullshit! Which one? That is so cool!"

"What are you doing here anyway?" I asked, ignoring her questions.

"Well," she began as she pulled a few loose curls away from her face. "Thought you might want an escape from this prison."

"I'm grounded for life, remember?" I plopped down on my bed beside her and leaned my head on her shoulder.

"Not necessarily," she said in a sing-song voice.

"OK, spill!" I demanded, sitting up.

"At this very moment, my mum's trying to convince your dad to let you sleep over. She's not lying to him about you not leaving the house, but she's leaving out one insignificant detail."

"Insignificant, huh? Where did you get that word from?"

"Are you saying I'm dumb?" She looked at me sternly. Although she was younger than me, she always thought herself much older because of her height, mature looks, and experience with boys.

"More like implying," I replied with a giggle as she threw a pillow at me.

"Anyway, she's not telling your dad that we're having guests over for dinner and that they're also gonna be staying and watching some DVDs with us."

"You're not saying that ..."

"Yep!"

"But I broke up with Adrian. I told you about what happened on Monday."

"Puh-lease Tam. As if he's going to listen to you. He's crazy about you and has been bugging me to organise something much sooner, but I told him your dad never lets you out on school nights. By the way, where were you last night? You didn't answer my texts."

"Oh, I crashed early. Sorry, *habibi*." I turned my eyes away from hers. I could *not* tell her about my Friday night escape. She would get upset that I didn't spend the evening with her. I also didn't want to tell her about James: one, because of Adrian, and two, because nothing would eventuate anyway as I hadn't even decided if I wanted to go to his party. *You are going!*

"There is no way Dad is going to agree to this, you know. He hasn't talked to me since last Sunday. Not that I really care anyway." I shrugged my shoulders, stood up to open the door, and tried to eavesdrop on their conversation. As I tiptoed out of my room, Sara followed. My aunt came rushing upstairs and told me to get changed as Dad had agreed to let me go as long as I was home in time for church tomorrow morning. I flew at my aunt, gave her a warm hug, and thanked her over and over. *Oh God. Calm down. It's not that big of a deal.*

I changed quickly and threw pyjamas, makeup, and my diary into my backpack. I thanked my dad on our way. He just made an "I'm not pleased about this" sound and waved me away. Sara and I skipped down the driveway with our arms linked, belting out *It's My Life* by Bon Jovi.

When we arrived at Sara's house, I rushed into her room, applied some makeup, and ran the straightener through my hair.

"Where'd your mum go, Sara?"

"Out with her man," Sara replied, touching up her eyes with another layer of mascara.

"Do you two get along?"

"Yeah, he's awesome. Hurry up! They're gonna be here any minute."

"Do I look OK?"

"Sooo hot!" she gushed.

"I'm sooo nervous," I informed her, biting my lower lip.

"Why?" I looked away as she tried to meet my eyes.

"Well, I mean, come on, Sara. What if he wants to do more than just kiss? I know you and Shadi will give us alone time, and I'm scared shitless. I haven't had a boyfriend before, remember?'

"Little Tam, you are too cute!"

"Don't talk to me like I am a child!" I exclaimed, slapping her hand away as she was about to pinch my cheek.

"Geez, touchy!"

"Piss off, Sara." I turned away from her, walked out of her room, and headed down the stairs.

"Oh Tam, don't be like that," she called out as she followed me. "I was just being typical silly me. You know I don't see you as a child. God, you are the most intelligent sixteen year old I know. I just find your innocence cute. That's all. I mean, I haven't slept with Shadi or anything, but we have fooled around, and it isn't that scary. You just have to learn to be comfortable around Adrian."

"I know …" I sighed and plopped down on her couch just as the doorbell rang. Sara squealed and ran towards the door. She gave Adrian a peck on the cheek and then passionately and unabashedly kissed Shadi. *Get a freaking room.* Adrian gave me a quick kiss on the lips as he sat next to me. We ordered pizza and chatted about school and work. All of them had part-time jobs except me, as my father did not believe I was old enough to carry such a "position of responsibility". Adrian and Shadi told us about all the wogs who hang out at their work, Bell Street Macas, with their spruced up cars and gelled hair.

"I just admire their cars. Beautiful machinery, you know," Adrian stated.

"What is it about that hangout that attracts them?" I asked, rolling my eyes.

"It's a way of them proving who they are and what they represent," Shadi replied, shrugging his shoulders.

"And what's that? Heroes and sick dudes because they own hotted up cars and have too much product in their hair."

"Tam, you're a bit harsh on your own kind. Why do you diss Lebos so badly?" Adrian asked.

"Because they are Marios! Dickheads! They think that being like that will cover the fact that they can't express themselves in a grammatically correct manner and that they will never be anyone of significance." As I finished my sentence I raised my eyes to find all three of them staring at me in utter bewilderment.

"Now that was majorly harsh," Adrian muttered almost inaudibly.

"I agree, and I'm sure Shadi does, too," Sara added as Shadi nodded. "You look at your brother and your cousins, Tam, and generalise their behaviour to all Lebo guys. It's mean, and it's not right.'

"Sorry, I didn't mean to sound so bitchy and pretentious. Sorry, Shadi. You know I would never think of *you* in that way."

"It's cool. Just give us all a chance to prove we can be better than the way we are portrayed in society and the media," Shadi replied.

I sighed, grabbed my glass, and walked towards the kitchen. I knew my opinions were biased and harsh because of my screwed up family, and I didn't mean to sound so opinionated. I just knew that so many young Lebos (including a few of my cousins) smoked weed and wasted away the best years of their youth. They got into brawls, received criminal records, and hindered any chance of a good future. I wondered if I was just mirroring my dad's opinions. *You sure are! Just go away. Leave me alone!*

"You OK?" Adrian asked as he walked into the kitchen.

"Yeah," I replied, intertwining my fingers though his. "I'm just an idiot with a big mouth sometimes. Actually, most of the time," I said, rolling my eyes as he laughed.

"Just count to ten before you speak, or …" he mumbled leaning down and kissing me softly. As my lips moulded themselves to his, he pushed my body closer. We finally pulled away, both catching our breaths. I filled my glass with Coke and offered him the rest of the can. He took it and headed back to the lounge room as I made some microwave popcorn. Sara and Shadi had disappeared. Adrian put a DVD on, and we sat close together on the couch, sharing the popcorn. We watched the whole movie without pashing, and I was proud of his self-control. All he did was hold my hand and stroke my face from time to time.

"Tell me about your family," I asked him as I switched off the plasma.

"Not much to tell."

"Come on. I want to know more about you." I started running my fingers through his curls.

"OK … uh … my older brother is nothing like me. He can't sit down and read anything, even if someone paid him. He loves cars and is gonna open his own shop soon. My little sister worries me because she's too pretty and naive. She turns thirteen next week, and the older she gets, the more protective I become. Not the crazy type protective," he stated as I raised my eyebrows.

"I'm sure she loves that you are her big brother. I, on the other hand, would trade my little brother for a rat if I could." He laughed and kissed me on the lips.

I pulled away, "Um Age, are we like exclusive? I mean like boyfriend, girlfriend?"

"Hell, yeah!" he replied and kissed me passionately. Adrian made me want him even more because he would only touch my face and my hair. He was the perfect gentleman, and I hoped he wouldn't stay that way for too much longer.

CHAPTER 5

THE NEXT MORNING, I WAS on a happy high and found it difficult to sleep in. On the way back home, I couldn't help thinking about James as well as Adrian. I was annoyed at myself for being silly and immature. James was so hot and independent and had his own place! If I ever had to run away from home, he would be my knight in shining armour. I could live with him if need be. *You are so naive!* I shook my head and walked through my front door. As I headed to the bathroom, my brother walked past with just a towel around his waist, and I looked away with irritation. *Ew!*

"What?" he slurred as I rolled my eyes and turned to say hello to my father as he walked up the corridor.

"Tamara."

"Yes, Dad?" I replied as I turned to face him.

"I hope you behaved yourself last night?" He always looked at me like a prosecutor would stare down a defendant, itching for the defendant to confirm that he was lying.

"Yes, I did."

"You better have shown your aunt the respect she deserves," he stated with a frown as his eyebrows almost touched each other.

"Of course, Dad. I always do." Shit! Was I overdoing it? Please, please do not keep staring at me like that. *Just be cool.* I headed towards the bathroom. He touched my shoulder, and I turned to face him once again.

"I just want you to be able to lift your head up high and make me proud in the eyes of my family," he informed me as he pinched my cheek. I smiled awkwardly and almost fell over in my hurry to get inside the bathroom. *What. The. Hell!* He never showed me any physical affection. As I looked at my reflection in the mirror, I scrutinised my eyes. How could he not see that I was as guilty as sin? *I guess my petite, angelic features could be deceiving. But you shouldn't let him fool you. Dad gives affection and takes it away just as quickly.*

The saddest memory of my childhood was when I was five years old and making Mum a cup of tea. As I was carrying the sugar bowl, it slipped out of my hands and shattered on the floor. I looked down and started crying uncontrollably at the thought of what Dad would do to me for breaking it. He yelled at first and called me a clumsy little fool. Then when he saw the state I was in, he told me to stop crying and to just clean up the mess. I was shocked and relieved but also furious at myself for crying like a baby.

Sighing, I willed the memory away and looked in the mirror, thinking again how weird Dad's behaviour was just then and shrugged my shoulders, flicked away my dark brown hair, and started getting ready for church.

★ ★ ★

After Sunday Mass, I spent the day in my room trying to come up with an original and inspiring short story for the writing competition. I procrastinated for as long as possible and finally started typing. I wrote 2,000 words in two hours. I messaged Fi and Mariam and reminded them to bring DVDs when they came over for dinner.

My mum made my favourite for dinner, tabouli, and this spice-filled rice and lamb dish with pine nuts, almonds, and chestnuts.

She also added hommus and baba ghanouj to the feast because we had guests and she loved showing off her cooking skills. My father interrogated Mariam and Fiona about their future plans and how they should aim to become doctors. I rolled my eyes and kicked their legs under the table. They stifled their giggles, and as soon as we ran into my bedroom, we burst out laughing.

"God! He sounds like a broken record. Sorry, besties!"

"It's OK. My mum does the same thing," Mariam replied with irritation as she plopped down on my bed. Fiona took out her nail kit and started painting my toenails.

"Should we do hands?" she asked.

"Nah … Miss Mitchell will just get out the acetone and make us take it off," Mariam replied.

"Stupid strict Catholic school!" I exclaimed.

'How is Adrian, Tam?' Fi asked mischievously.

"How is Tony, Fi?' I retorted.

"Same old … no progress whatsoever! Whenever he visits with his family, we rarely get any time alone. He always runs the other way as soon as my dad walks into the room. How am I ever going to get him truly alone?" she wailed, burying her face into my pillow.

"And what would you do if you could?" Mariam asked with a raised eyebrow.

"Use your imagination, Mariam!" I replied with a devious smile.

"You are disgusting," Mariam replied, finishing off her blood-red toenails.

"And you are just jealous because you can't even speak to your green-eyed hottie."

"Ohhh, Tam is so superior now that she has a boyfriend," Mariam cooed.

"Oh my gawd! Like your face is so totally turning green right now," I retorted, shoving her off my bed. Fi and I laughed at her as she made sure her toenails weren't ruined.

"Bitch!" Mariam muttered.

"Right back at ya, Mi Mi!"

"Argh!" She walked out of my room and into the bathroom, and Fi and I simultaneously rolled our eyes at her melodramatic nature, knowing she would calm down sooner or later.

"Fi, just meet Tony after school one day," I suggested, touching the black polish on my toes to see if it was dry.

"Easier said than done," Fi replied.

'Well, how about we double date? I can say we need to go to Academic and General in the city to get a few novels for English next term. How about Wednesday?'

"Really? But what about Mi Mi?" Fiona replied.

"We'll run it past her." Eventually, she came back inside, and after much consoling from the both of us, she acknowledged us again.

"So Mi Mi, do you wanna go with us to the movies Wednesday after school?"

"You're bringing your boys, right?" Mariam asked.

"Yeah I'm trying to set Fi up with Tony."

"And what? I'm just going to happily be the fifth wheel?"

"I'll ask Age to bring a friend," I suggested, smiling.

"I'd rather burn in hell than be a charity case!" Mariam replied with a frown.

"OK, sorry I mentioned it," I replied as I started to believe that she *was* really jealous. I had to set this girl up with a guy soon, or she was going to continuously be a cranky bitch. As soon as Mariam and Fiona left, I sat on my bed, staring up the ceiling and stressing about Wednesday. I was hesitant about whether we should go. After all, there would be many people who might see us in the city. I convinced myself that I had as much right to live my life as any other teenager. That said, if I got caught again, any contact with the outside world would cease to exist. Dad would probably have me home schooled as punishment.

★ ★ ★

Wednesday finally arrived, and we met at the tram stop a few blocks away from school. We all exchanged pleasantries, and Adrian held my hand and tried to kiss me on the lips, but I turned my face. *Gutless!* I was still embarrassed to show affection in public! What if people could see that I was an amateur kisser? Besides, the inescapable fear of getting caught never subsided. I snuggled up to Adrian on the tram, and he lightly kissed my forehead.

As we got off at Elizabeth Street, I scanned the crowd and sighed with relief as I didn't recognise anyone. Then again, Lebanese people are like CIA agents, lurking in the crowds, inconspicuous, scanning all the teenage girls so they could then gossip about their actions to the rest of the Lebanese community. Inevitably that gossip would reach the ears of that particular girl's family. *Maybe Dad should find out. It would speed up the likelihood of a heart attack.* I sighed with frustration, and Fiona looked at me quizzically. I just shrugged my shoulders. A friendship like ours imparted an unspoken understanding. We walked into Village Cinemas on Russel Street, and the guys agreed to watch a romantic comedy. I smiled appreciatively as Adrian headed straight towards the candy bar to buy me popcorn. Fiona had to suggest this to Tony, and as she raised her eyebrows in my direction, I stifled a giggle. Tony hadn't yet held her hand or even looked at her properly, and I wondered when he would man up and finally show his attraction towards her.

This time, we pashed quite a few times during the movie, and I heard Tony clearing his throat uncomfortably. I kept poking Fiona, but she wouldn't make the first move. Who could blame her? Finally, Tony abruptly grabbed her hand, and they leaned over and kissed. I tried not to grimace as their teeth clattered against each other knowing how humiliating that feels. Adrian and I stopped pashing as not to miss the ending of the movie. Tony and Fiona continued kissing, oblivious to the world around them, and I was happy to be witness to her first kiss.

We walked to Melbourne Central and had lunch at the food court. Once again, the boys paid for everything, and Fiona and I smirked at one another, both glad that we had such gallant boyfriends. Tony did most of the talking as we bombarded him with questions about his village in Italy and what he had to do to get a visa to stay in Australia. Adrian and Tony compared village stories that had Fiona and me in hysterics. We walked back to the train station and said our goodbyes. I gave Adrian a quick peck on the lips. I glanced over at Fiona and was surprised to see her kissing Tony passionately.

"You have an issue with PDA, don't you?"

"PDA?"

"Yeah, public displays of affection."

"Oh … mmm … maybe," I replied turning away blushing. He grabbed my chin and turned my face back towards him. *Aggressive, I like.*

"I'll help you get over that," he said as he leaned over and kissed me unabashedly. I kissed him back, trying to balance my weight on the tips of my school shoes.

"I'll text you tonight," he muttered against my lips. I said goodbye to Tony and Fiona said ciao to Adrian. I almost tripped over my two left feet stepping onto the train.

"Wow! He even has an effect on your feet," Fiona said while giggling. I punched her arm in retaliation.

"You should not be making fun of me, missy! Thanks to me, you got with Tony and experienced your first kiss."

"Yeah, I know … like oh my God!" she gushed. We giggled and gossiped over our boys the whole way home. Fiona stayed over for dinner, and we discussed the ridiculous amount of reading we had to complete both for English and debating. My parents nodded approvingly, and we poked each other under the table, ecstatic that we had gotten away with our lies.

CHAPTER 6

THE FOLLOWING DAY, ADRIAN SENT me a text after school telling me to meet him at the park. I asked if anything was wrong. He simply replied, "Just meet me there in thirty minutes!" I called Mum and explained that I was getting some extra help from my maths teacher and that I would be running an hour or so late. As I walked towards him, his back was facing me and I put my arms around his waist.

"Promise me you won't freak out."

"What do you mean?" I asked trying to turn him around to face me.

"Just promise!" he replied tersely.

"OK … I promise." He turned his face slowly towards me, and I gasped as I saw the cut on the left side of his lips and his black eye.

"What … what … happened?"

"Your cousin Rami and his brother. They were waiting for me outside school."

"What the fuck! How dare they!"

"You promised you wouldn't freak out," he interrupted.

"Well, that was before I knew what they did! I am going to kill them!" *I will get my hands on a cricket bat, and I will make their knuckles bleed so badly that they will think twice about using them against Adrian again!*

"Tam, please, don't say or do anything. You will just make things worse."

"I can't just stand by and allow them to beat you up and get away with it. Fucking arrogant, violent Lebos! And you wonder why I don't associate with my own kind. The way they think 'fists first' is the only way to handle all confronting situations. Why today? Did they see us yesterday?"

"Someone had obviously told Rami. He said he wasn't gonna say anything to your dad because you were still doing what you wanted. He said that this would hopefully make me stay away from you. I gave him a black eye, as well, but having both of them at me at the same time was tough. I wish I had known they were coming. I would have brought a cousin, too," he informed me with a smile. Then he groaned and touched his lip.

"Did they hurt you anywhere else? Is there anything broken?" I asked while caressing his face with my fingertips.

"Nothing is broken. Just bruises," he replied and leaned down to kiss me softly.

"I bet they wouldn't have bashed you up if you were Lebo!"

"Don't worry about them anymore, Tam," he replied as I held him close. He groaned and touched his ribs, and I quickly pulled away.

"Sorry ..."

"It's OK. Come here," he muttered as he caressed the side of my face and kissed me again. I pulled away and looked deep into his eyes. How could I express the depths of my feelings for him at that moment? Was I in love? Was it way too early to be in love? Seeing him hurt like this broke my heart, and I knew if it wasn't love I was experiencing, it was surely something very close to it.

"What are we gonna do?" I asked leaning my head on his shoulder.

"Don't know, Tam. But your cousins are deluding themselves if they think a few bruises will stop me from seeing you. It's actually had the opposite effect," he said with a smirk.

"You are unbelievable! You find this situation amusing, and I find it *so* infuriating," I stated stomping my foot in the ground.

'Really, Tam. It's all good. Chillax."

"No, it's not all good, Adrian! I can't just chillax! Rami will tell my dad, and things *will* get worse. He will probably leave work early and pick me up from school every day, and we won't see each other at all!" *That will only happen when hell freezes over!*

"Maybe not. Let's just wait and see, OK?"

"OK," I replied as I hugged him gently.

★ ★ ★

That night when Dad arrived home, I was setting the table for dinner. He muttered hello and went straight to the couch and sat where his body was permanently engraved in its cushions. We ate dinner mostly in silence, both my parents interrupting occasionally to voice their concern over the continuous political battles portrayed on the Arabic channels. My brother and I rolled our eyes when they weren't looking and remained silent. After all, Lebanon was their country, not ours. I suddenly realised that as a family, we rarely spoke. When we did, our conversations revolved mostly around politics, and the majority of the time, Charlie and I refused to contribute.

I watched my parents before heading to my room. My mother was reading the acclaimed horoscope book by this blond Lebanese lady. Seriously, she believed every word that woman predicted. It was a bit sad. Dad was watching the news, engrossed as usual by the latest political rant. *Why does he care?* I continued to stare at my parents. They had become roommates, and it was so sad to see. I felt sorry for my mum. Dad had work to keep him busy. What did she have? Nothing but looking after us.

Before going to sleep, I spent an hour talking with Adrian about my dreams of becoming a writer and he revealed his dreams of becoming a lawyer. My heart would miss a beat when I thought I heard someone lurking outside my room, but when I opened the door, no one was in sight. We finally wished each other goodnight. As I hung up the phone, I realised he was the ray of sunlight in this dark prison cell I was in. My crime? Being born a female in a Christian Lebanese family and having strong feminist values. Or even just not wanting to miss out on the joys of teenage love.

CHAPTER 7

THE NEXT DAY, ADRIAN AND I had an argument on Facebook chat during my computer class. His mum had made him stay home from school until she could have answers about who had caused his black eye. I suggested we take a break so that my cousins wouldn't go after him again. The conversation turned nasty as he thought I was indirectly calling him a coward! Puh-lease! Why do guys twist the things you say? I thought only girls did that. I tried to explain to him that was so not what I meant and then he demanded I be honest and just break up with him if that was my intention. I started getting really peeved. *You shouldn't have asked for a break, idiot!* I didn't know how to respond to his sudden temper tantrum, and our words were getting misinterpreted. I wished more than anything we had started this conversation in person. Just when I wanted to set things straight, the bell rang and I had to sign off. I said I would talk to him later, and he replied that I shouldn't bother trying to call him as he wouldn't pick up. I slammed the keyboard in exasperation and headed to my next class. What an immature annoying ... argh! *But he is so hot. Wait until we make up; the sex will be amazing! Oh yeah, I'm not ready ...* As I walked to English class, I thought about James's party and decided to go. *You are just getting even at Adrian for chucking a fit. But no complaints here, as James is a total babe! Who am I becoming?*

"So I heard your Italian Stallion got a bit of a bruising?" Rania said, interrupting my hazy reverie as she appeared alongside me in front of the classroom door.

"How did you hear about that?"

"I have my sources," she replied with an evil smirk.

"What's your problem, Rania?"

"You are, fucking little angel! Miss Virgin Mary! You're a fucking coward! You say you hate being Lebanese but you still follow their rules," she replied as she picked at a fluff on the sleeve of my school jumper.

"I have no idea what I've done to upset you, but why don't you just tell me so I can get to class."

'Fucking grow up, daddy's little girl! Stew on that for a while!"

"Rania …"

"Shut up!" she interrupted. I tried to reply, but she had already stormed into class. *That girl needs some serious psychiatric help or maybe a slap right across her smug face!*

★ ★ ★

Friday night, I lied to my parents for the hundredth time, not only about a debating meeting but also dinner afterwards. They believed me as I forged a letter from my debating teacher and even managed to get the school letterhead on there. I would make an exceptional CIA agent! I wore jeans and a plain cotton top, but hid a short skirt and a low-cut top (borrowed from Sara) in my large handbag. After Dad dropped me off at the State Library, I rushed to the bathroom, changed, and applied some make-up. As I left the library, the security guard watched me walk away with a puzzled look. *Yep, buddy: I am the same chick, just much hotter!*

I tapped my heels together the whole tram ride to James's and tried not to bite my nails. I noticed a bunch of guys checking out my legs, and I cleared my throat and turned away from them. They started snickering and whispering dirty words in Arabic. People always mistook me for Italian, and it worked to my advantage right then. They started betting who could pick me up, and one even had the audacity to state that he could get as far as second base with me right there on the tram. Thankfully, my stop came before either of them approached me. As I walked down the stairs, I turned around and told them good night and to have a good evening in Arabic. The expression on their faces was priceless! I smiled to myself as I walked down Bouverie Street.

I was so nervous walking up the stairs to James's dorm. I knocked softly on his door, waited for a few long torturous moments, and then knocked again. My eyes finally adjusted enough to see the small note just below my nose stating that the party was outside in the barbeque area. I sighed and wondered if I should just bail. *No freaking way!*

I walked back down the stairs, ready to bolt out of there. As I turned the corner, I slammed into someone's chest.

"Hey!" James said in a very loud voice, leaning over and giving me a quick peck on the cheek.

"Hi," I replied.

"Was starting to think you weren't gonna make it. I did say seven, yeah?"

"You did, but I had to go home and change out of my school uniform and catch public transport to get here."

"Oh yeah, I forget you are still in high school. Shit! Exams are soon. You scared shitless yet?"

"Bad! I just can't wait until they're over, but then I will be worrying about my ATAR …"

"You'll be alright. Just give me a sec, and I'll be right back."

"Sure," I replied watching him bolt up the stairs. He came back a few minutes later and led me towards the party. He instantly placed a cruiser in my hand and introduced me to some of his friends. I started chatting to an Aussie-Indian girl, and we were soon comparing crazy strict parent stories. James went back to the esky and came back with more drinks. One of his friends circled the party with a tray of shotties. I took the one that James offered me, and it didn't taste as bad as I thought it would. The music suddenly got louder, and James grabbed my hand and led me to the dance floor. I was so self-conscious, and I knew that I looked like a moron! I sighed with relief when a slow song came on, expecting James to lead me away, but instead he placed his hands around my waist, and I *had* to place mine around his neck. I felt awkward, uncomfortable, and way out of my league. I looked anywhere but at him and found some of his female friends smiling warmly in our direction. Had he told them about me?

"Having fun?"

"Yep," I muttered forcing myself to meet his eyes.

"I really am glad you made it tonight," he stated with his adorable smile. He then brought my body closer to his and rested his face near mine. I was trying to control my heart so that it would not beat right out of my chest. As soon as the song ended, he took my hand, got some drinks, and continued to lead me to his dorm room. I had to hold on to the rails, and it wasn't because of the heels; I was quite tipsy. I didn't know what to do. If I let go of his hand, he would see it as a rejection, but then again, what was he expecting to happen up there? *Use your imagination!*

As I followed him into his room, the first thing that caught my eye was how tidy it was. I guess guys learn to clean up after themselves when they live alone. I reckon Charlie would make mum clean his place once a week if he had to live on his own. It was a small room, but it fit a desk, a single bed, and a bar fridge. I looked down at the bed and wondered how many other girls he had brought up here. He sat down in the middle of his bed, and I stayed standing glancing around, pretending to be interested in all his pictures and trophies. He asked for my number and typed it in his phone. I turned away again, and as I smiled at a picture of him holding a footy, he cleared his throat. When I turned back towards him, I found him standing very close to me. He smiled that irresistible smile and leaned over. I closed my eyes, instantly willing this moment away, and intentionally dropped my phone. The noise made him start. I bent over to pick it up.

"James, I need to get going."

"Why? Stay … It's early … Just one kiss …" He muttered as he held me tightly. I realised that James was fairly drunk and probably high, as I had seen him share a joint with his mates. *And? So what?*

"I think you're slightly drunk, and I don't really wanna do anything …"

He swayed slightly as he tried to shrug nonchalantly.

"Whatevs," he muttered as he headed towards the door.

"You're not angry with me, are you?"

"Nah," was the only response I received, and I shook my head with irritation as I followed him down the stairs.

★ ★ ★

When I got home, I rushed to the backyard and quickly put my top and jeans over my skirt and skimpy top. As soon as I walked through the door, I told my parents that I was dead tired, and went straight to bed. As I started taking off my top, I held it to my nose and realised that it smelt like James's aftershave. As soon as I placed my head on the pillow, the world spun and I felt slightly ill. I sat up in bed and waited until my parents went to sleep. I tiptoed into the kitchen and made myself a sandwich and drank a lot of water. I instantly felt better, and when I laid back down, the dizziness had subsided. My thoughts were muddled. It was true the night ended badly, but I still couldn't believe I had attended a Uni party tonight. Me! The nerd. The shyest girl in my year level. I had almost kissed a Melbourne Uni student in his dorm room. I thought about how Mariam and Fiona were going to freak! But could I tell them? What about Adrian? I fell asleep as all these thoughts swirled around my head.

★ ★ ★

The next day, I woke up to the sound of raised voices. I walked into the living room just as my aunt was slamming the door shut behind her.

"What's wrong, Mum?" I asked as I walked towards her.

"*Mashe,* nothing," she replied, avoiding eye contact.

"Mum, seriously."

"Please, leave it alone," she interrupted sternly as I watched her eyes fill with tears. She walked towards her bedroom, and I proceeded to clean up the kitchen and the rest of the house. She didn't come out of her room until dinner time. *Maybe she stopped taking her antidepressants!* Mum prepared dinner in silence as I sat at the living room table working on my maths homework. I hated both the subject and the teacher. Seriously, why would I need algebra in the future? What's the point of making me try to learn these stupid equations? I had told my teacher as much, and she had given me a ten-minute lecture on the importance of blah blah … I had tuned her out and then replied that there was no way I was ever going to learn these useless equations. She replied that if I didn't change my attitude towards maths in general, I would never pass her class.

Such a typical teacher response. Why couldn't a teacher, just once, simply whisper to me in the strictest confidence, "I get ya, chicks! If you can't get your head around it, don't bother. You are more than welcome to continue reading novels in my class, and I will pass you. At least you're improving your vocabulary instead of reading trashy magazines." *Keep dreaming.*

I shook my head out of my fantasy world and watched my mum as she occasionally rubbed at her eyes. It had been ages since I'd seen her as upset as this. When Dad came home, he sensed her mood straight away but chose to ignore it and her. I wondered if they had gotten into a fight last night. Charlie was out and about as usual, and no one seemed to care that he missed family dinners. I would get chided every time I missed just one. *So unfair and sexist and just plain screwed up!*

★ ★ ★

I spent the first part of the evening watching romantic movies that depressed me even more. I wondered why girls intensified their depression by listening to depressing songs (which dare I admit I have done) or by watching sappy romantic movies. After my movie marathon, I chatted with Fi and Mariam on Facebook chat. I hoped that Adrian would log on, but he didn't. I chatted for ages with Fiona about our boys as we felt sorry for ourselves because we knew a repeat of Wednesday was highly unlikely. Mariam kept asking me what we were chatting about, and when I told her, she showed signs of jealousy again. I would have felt left out, too, if I were the only one without a boyfriend, and I vowed to set her up with someone soon. But how and when … I finally logged off at midnight and read *Romeo and Juliet* for an hour before finally closing my exhausted eyes and thinking back to the time when I would help out at Dad's restaurant on the weekends as I wasn't allowed to go anywhere else. I'd been forbidden to go to parties and sleepovers and camps like the rest of the girls in my year level. At the age of fourteen, I knew life couldn't get any more depressing. I was pitting olives for pizza and not doing a very good job of it. Dad lost it, taking his anger over one of his incompetent employees out on me. I bolted to the bathroom before he could embarrass me even more. My sobs were preventing me from breathing. I banged my forehead on the tiled wall, wishing I could be anywhere else. After composing myself, I went back to pitting olives, and a very cute boy walked in with his family. He smiled at me, and I smiled back. There was a pinball machine and a pool table on the upper level to keep kids amused so that their parents could dine in peace. I headed upstairs and smiled flirtatiously at the gorgeous boy. I stood there and pretended to play the pinball machine while constantly looking over at the door. He finally walked in and headed to the pool table. After a few moments, he turned to me and asked what my score was.

"Uh," I began. I wasn't even playing. "I'm not that good at this thing, and anyway, I don't have any change," I informed him as I smiled and looked up at him.

"I'll teach you," he replied, standing behind me and placing a dollar coin in the machine. He put his hands over mine and guided them to the buttons. He instructed me on how to play, and even after I knew what to do, his hands didn't leave mine. When I squealed with excitement after winning, I turned around and beamed up at him. He smiled back, and after a few long and tortuous moments, he leaned over and gave me a peck on the lips. At that very moment, Dad walked in. He pulled the boy away from me and slapped me right across the face. I was mortified and hated him then more than ever before. Dad ordered the boy to stay away from me, and he took me straight home, forbidding me from ever working at the restaurant again. I didn't even know the boy's name, but his kiss kept me on a happy high for days. I couldn't get him out of my mind, but there was no possible way I would ever see him again. I guessed he was the reason I was so attracted to James. They had an uncanny resemblance to one another. Everyone has a doppelganger in this world, right?

★ ★ ★

The following day, Sara texted me and told me she was coming over. I called her and told her about what had happened the day before with our mums and suggested she get her mum to come over for lunch, as well. Dad was home, so Mum and Dad were civil to one another. After lunch, we went to my room and chatted about school and our guys. I didn't tell her about James, because I knew she would scold me for being so stupid and treating Shadi's best mate like crap. My father went to his friend's place to play cards, and Sara and I tried to overhear our mothers' conversation.

"Leila, I'm sorry for being so pushy yesterday," my aunt said in Arabic. They found it much easier to communicate with one another in their first language.

"I'm sorry for being so sensitive. Lydia, you know that I can't just leave him. You know I would never do that to Tamara and Charlie. Especially Tamara. But I'm just so lonely," she said as she lit a cigarette.

'I know, my sister, but you can't continue being this miserable either."

"Yes, I can. It's a sacrifice I'm willing to make for my children. And besides, if I leave, you know what could happen. He will exploit me.'

"You're right," my aunt replied as Sara and I gave each other a puzzled look.

"WTF?" I said to Sara.

"I know," Sara replied with shock. We tiptoed back upstairs and came bolting back down, chatting loudly. Both women paused abruptly and smiled at us. We watched one of our favourite movies of all time, *The Notebook*, and pigged out on junk food. The sisters shared a secret glance before my aunt and Sara said their goodbyes. I motioned with my hand for her to text me if she heard anything and she nodded that I do the same. I tried to talk to Mum again, but she was in a leave-me-alone mood. So I did and went to sleep, wondering if Adrian was ever going to talk to me again.

CHAPTER 8

THE NEXT WEEK WENT BY slowly and mundanely. Adrian finally messaged me Friday during school, asking to meet him at Sara's house tomorrow since Shadi was going over for dinner and a DVD. I replied that I couldn't wait to see him. Ten minutes later, James texted me and "Sorry, babe, about last Friday. I was bit drunk but would like to see you again soon." I didn't reply as I wanted him to squirm for a while. I asked my parents if I could go over Sara's again for a DVD night, and to my great astonishment, they agreed. I suspected they were still arguing as they seemed preoccupied. As I left the room, they turned back towards the Arabic news. *Seriously, don't come to Australia if all you are going to worry about is your home country. It's like the only reason they are living here is to give us a great education and future, but they are ignoring their own happiness.*

The next night while waiting for *khalto* Lydia to pick me up, I watched the news with them for a while, just so they couldn't keep saying we never spent any quality time together. I asked Dad a question about the current politics and instantly regretted it as he kept blabbing on about it until he heard the car horn. My parents were very passionate about what had happened to their country. They believed all religions were equal and should live in harmony, and if all Lebanese people thought that way, there wouldn't be so much civil unrest.

* * *

I was nervous as my aunt dropped us off at her place and went off to her party. Sara and I waited for the boys to arrive. They eventually did, and Sara and Shadi didn't hesitate to start with the PDA. Adrian and I just exchanged awkward hellos. We ordered pizza and chatted about school. We ate in silence at the kitchen table until Sara motioned to Shadi to follow her upstairs. I looked across at Adrian and saw him staring at me.

"Hey," he muttered, leaning in closer and giving me a peck on the cheek.

"Hey," I replied, and without a moment's hesitation, I kissed him passionately on the lips. After about five minutes, we finally pulled away, and I leaned my head on his shoulder.

"I'm sorry about last week. I was just angry because I thought you wanted to give up on us."

"No, it wasn't that at all."

"I know. Sara told Shadi, and he told me," he interrupted with a smirk.

"Can't anyone keep secrets these days?" I muttered, annoyed.

"I'm sure you can forgive her this time," he said.

"Yeah, whatevs," I replied, running my fingers through his hair.

"Just promise me that you won't!"

"Won't what?"

"Give up."

"I promise. But Age, honestly, why are you putting up with all this shit? Why me?" *Why must you always talk so much?*

"You are crazy, you know that?" he replied, pushing my head closer towards his and kissing me with more passion than I had ever felt from him before.

"Wow," I finally managed to whisper, "you keep kissing me like that, and we might have to take this somewhere more private."

"Really?"

"Uh huh!" I replied with a sheepish smile. He held my hand and led me to the living room. He sent Shadi a text, waited for his response, and started kissing me. *This is more like it!*

"What did you just send him?" I asked, pulling away and trying to catch my breath.

"To message me before they come downstairs," he replied and then continued to kiss me. One hand reached under my top, while the other snuck its way up my thigh. As Adrian kissed me and I experienced a guy's touch for the first time in my life, guilty feelings kept seeping their way into my conscious thoughts. I tried to chase them away. It was so difficult for me to just enjoy my time with Adrian when my conscience was constantly badgering me about "needing to stay a good Catholic girl" and "what would your dad do if he found you like this" and so on and so forth. I didn't really care though, did I? I mean, if I did, I wouldn't be here, right? *Why shouldn't you be able to enjoy being a teenager like everybody else?* Fuck it! If I lost my virginity to Adrian, at least I would make sure we would at least have admitted our love to one another beforehand. That was enough for me. That was what I had always vowed to myself and to God: that I would not share such intimacy with any guy unless I loved him. *That is what you say now, but just wait.*

Shadi and Sara finally made it back downstairs and brought with them a bottle of vodka. I looked at all three of them sceptically. Were they serious? They opened the bottle and started passing it between them. It finally reached me, and I hesitated.

"Come on, Tam. Live a little," Sara said with a smirk. I took a gulp and then dry heaved. Shadi laughed as he hit my back while I coughed. Straight vodka was disgusting! We then moved to the backyard and shared a cigarette. Shadi brought out a joint. I didn't say anything. I just waited for Adrian's reaction. He took it from Shadi, lit it, and inhaled deeply.

"Just a small puff," he ordered as he passed it to me. I didn't listen, and I took drag after drag as it was passed around our little circle.

Half an hour later, we were all giggling and eating all the junk food in the house. I could not stop kissing Adrian, and my PDA issue flew out the window, along with all my other inhibitions. I still could not believe I had smoked marijuana.

"I guess everyone drinks and does weed these days," I stated.

"Yeah, drugs and booze have been at every party I've ever been to," Adrian replied.

"But it's sad to start at such a young age," I said.

"Only if you are addicted, Tam. Shadi and I don't do this often."

"Still …" In a way, I guess I was just disappointed with what was happening to the world. With each passing generation, kids were doing all this stuff at a younger and younger age. I suddenly felt cold and shuddered while Adrian put his arm around me, rubbing my shoulder. He truly was the best boyfriend a girl could ever wish for. A few minutes later, I rushed to the toilet and threw up everything I had eaten. Adrian held my hair back even after I yelled at him to leave me the fuck alone. He took care of me, and we laughed at how weak I was. He said that was what he loved about me.

"So you're saying that you like that I'm a weak shit?"

"No, I'm saying you're inexperienced, and I'm loving experiencing everything with you," he said handing me a chewy.

"Thanks, but I need to brush my teeth first," I stated sticking my tongue out at him.

"You are so loveable, Tam," he stated, looking deep into my eyes in the mirror as I brushed my teeth with my finger. I gargled and spat, wondering how he could say something like that when I looked the way I did. I wasn't sure if I was meant to say anything back. He leaned over, kissed me lightly on the lips, said his goodbyes, and walked out the door with Shadi.

"Oh my *God*! I heard that! Ahhh!" Sara squealed while I once again put my head in my hands and groaned.

CHAPTER 9

SUNDAY MORNING, I GOT UP and made myself a big breakfast. I then checked my email and found one from the writing competition. I stared at my inbox for ten minutes, scared to open the email, scared of rejection. Once I had built up the courage and clicked the email, I discovered that much to my disbelief, I had won the competition. It was the best piece I had ever written, but I had a read some of the other entries, and a few were written by University students. I was so happy I texted James and said that hopefully we could catch up again soon. I also texted Adrian to let him know that I won. *I think you like juggling two guys at once. Ahhh! Be quiet!*

I waited for the family lunch to announce my news just as Charlie had decided to grace us with his presence.

"I am glad, daughter, that you won. Very good, but do not let this affect your school work."

"Sure, Dad," I replied in English instead of Arabic to irritate him as much as he just annoyed me. Why on Earth would winning this competition affect my school work? *What is wrong with you? Can't you just be proud of me?*

"I am very happy to you, *habibti,* my darling," Mum said.

"It's *for* you, Mum, and Tam, why don't you be honest with Mum and Dad about everything, not just the good stuff?'

"What are you talking about, dipshit?"

"Do not talk to your brother that way, Tamara! Charlie, explain yourself."

"I think it would be best coming from Tamara."

"Seriously, Charlie. Just shut it!"

"Why don't you tell them what you have been up to other than the debating meetings, Tam?" He looked at me through squinted eyes, and I wondered what it was that I had done to prompt this sudden bout of wrath. *You didn't do anything; he must be high on weed or something!*

"Dad ... I have no idea."

"Bullshit!" he interrupted. "Dad, there is no debating! That finished ages ago. The only reason I am snitching on you, Tam, is because I heard you barfing when you got home last night. I'm not letting my sister run around like a slut getting drunk and God knows what else!'

"Why you little fu—"

"Tamara!" my father boomed, slamming his fist on the table. "Where were you last night?"

"I ... I ... was at a party."

"Did you drink?"

"I just had one drink, but I hadn't eaten much. That's why I got sick."

"Did you take drugs?"

"No!"

"Was that boy there?"

"No."

"I don't believe you!"

"I don't care *baba*, Dad! You think I am the worst daughter in the world because I went to a party and had one bloody drink!"

"Tamara, do ..." Dad tried to interrupt me, but I was seeing red! I knew I shouldn't say what I was about to say. I knew if I did, I would never have a good relationship with my brother, and he would never trust me again, but he gave me no reason to ever believe that I could ever trust *him* again. He had ratted me out without a moment's hesitation.

"He is the one who got his slut of a girlfriend pregnant! Your precious son here, the future star of soccer, is the irresponsible one, not me!" Everyone sat in silence for a few shocked moments.

"Is this true?"

"Yes, Dad," my brother answered with a death stare directed at me.

"I will give you money to take care of it," Dad stated without emotion. I stared incredulously at my father waiting for him to say more, do more, or to punish the little brat. We all just continued to sit there in silence until I stood up quickly, knocked over my chair, and stormed towards my room. This was not happening! *I knew there were major sexism issues in my culture, but this was just un-fucking-believable!*

Charlie could get away with murder just because he was male! I stared at my bedroom door with incredulity. My father finally knocked, opened the door, and stated that we were both grounded for the rest of the year. What a surprise! *Just throw that glass dolphin at the back of his head!*

I spent the rest of the day in my sanctuary. My mother brought my dinner on a tray, but would not meet my eyes. *Why is she so fucking scared of standing up for you?* I placed the tray outside my door as soon as I heard her walk down the stairs. I would starve myself to death and see how they would react! Ten minutes later, I took the tray back inside and gobbled down my dinner. I was starving.

★ ★ ★

Half an hour later, having signed off with Adrian on Facebook chat, who was more depressed than I was, something possessed me to message James. I asked him about his weekend. He messaged instantly and said it was good and asked what I was doing that night. I hesitated for a split second and replied that I was free. He asked me to come over, and I agreed. I knew my parents wouldn't try to speak to me tonight, and I knew Charlie and I would never speak again, so there was no chance of anyone finding out about my absence. I really couldn't explain why I went to see James instead of Adrian. Maybe I needed an outsider's opinion or just wanted to finally be honest with James about everything. Or maybe today's events made it impossible for me to think rationally. *Funny how you must always justify your actions.*

I got dressed as quietly as possible and wished I could sneak into the bathroom to brush my teeth. I put a chewy in my mouth, glanced at myself one final time in the mirror, and turned off my bedroom light. After sitting in darkness for ten minutes, I snuck out my bedroom window. Adrenaline engulfed me at that very moment. I felt like I could do anything and be anyone.

★ ★ ★

I took long deep breaths before I knocked on James's dorm room door. A girl walked out of the room beside his, smiled at me, and continued to walk down the stairs. I raised my hand to knock and lowered it again.

"You look hot, and he won't bite," she stated as she turned to look back up at me. I smiled back at her and wondered if I would ever be as confident as her when I became a Uni student. I knocked softly, and as soon as he opened the door, he grabbed my hand and pulled me inside. He slammed the door with his foot and gave me a warm hug. I pulled away and looked deep into his eyes. For a split second, I thought maybe I shouldn't be there, but a moment later, James leaned over and ran his fingers though my hair. His hand moved to my lips, and he lightly stroked my bottom lip with his fingertips. I was quivering inside, and my body felt like it was being slowly ignited. I wanted him to kiss me, but he just continued to stare into my eyes. I grabbed his hand and kissed his fingers. I moved his hand to my waist and leaned towards him. That was all the encouragement he needed. His other hand moved to my back and pushed my body closer towards him while his lips moulded themselves to mine. The kiss became passionate, and I felt his arousal through his pants.

"You're an amazing kisser," he whispered and leaned down to kiss me once again.

I let myself enjoy the experience, and I was soon lying on his bed, with his body crushing mine. His hand slid under my top and lightly grazed my bra. I could feel him fumbling around, trying to push my bra aside, and I didn't try to stop him. His lips touched the top of my left breast, and as I felt my first real sensual touch, I lost control. I kissed James so passionately that it felt as if our lips were glued to one another. He started rubbing his jeans against my skirt, and as my breathing quickened, my senses exploded. The heat moving to every inch of my body was intoxicating, and I didn't want him to stop what he was doing. For the first time in my life, my brain switched off and my senses took control. He groaned against my mouth as his movements became more intense. I wanted to take off my top, and I wanted my skin to touch his, but I didn't want to interrupt either. I let the warmth envelop me and moaned. When I opened my eyes and saw James looking at me with pure animalistic desire, I knew I had to stop before we went too far.

"James, I have to go," I stated, pushing him off me.

"Right now?" he muttered and proceeded to try pull me back down and give me a hickey.

"Stop! My dad will notice that." *So fucking what?*

"They don't let ya have a boyfriend?"

"Definitely not, and double no if he is a Uni student," I replied as I repositioned my clothing.

"I'm only a year older than you."

"Mmm … Actually, you are three years older than me."

"What?" he exclaimed, standing up and looking down at me.

"Yeah," I stood up and faced his wall with all his photos. "I am only in year ten. I didn't mean to lie to you, James, but I liked you."

"Fuck." He slumped down on his bed.

"I'm really sorry; I don't even know why I came here tonight. My dad's just grounded me for the rest of the year! God knows what will happen if he knows I wasn't home tonight."

"So you're only, what, like fifteen?"

"Sixteen," I replied not meeting his eyes.

"You're not Muslim, are you?"

"What difference would that make?" I asked, my eyes blazing.

"It would just make things worse if you were with an atheist like me, wouldn't it?" he replied, shrugging his shoulders.

"I guess, but no, I'm Catholic. But my dad is psycho strict, and although he just found out that my brother got his girlfriend pregnant and all I did was go to party and have a drink, we both received the same punishment."

"That's crazy!"

"Exactly my reaction."

"Ah, Tamara, that fact that you are sixteen and …"

I cut him off instantly. "I understand. You don't need to explain, James!" I sighed with exasperation.

"I mean your family, too," he mumbled, smiling at me sympathetically. I hated that! I hated people feeling sorry for me.

"Yeah, it's cool. I gotta go."

"Tamara, don't leave."

"It's fine James. I guess I should start getting used to this."

"Don't be like that. Your family will ease up."

"Yeah, when I'm an old maid! Anyway, I really have to go. Take care, James. Have a great life." I didn't mean to sound so bitter, but I couldn't help it. I was shitty at myself for coming here in the first place. He sent me a text on my way home saying that he was glad he had met me. He wished me a great life. I almost threw my mobile out the window of the tram, but instead deleted his message history and number.

★ ★ ★

The following day, I gave my father the silent treatment and only spoke when spoken to. It was what he had always taught me anyway. After dinner, my mum knocked softly on my door and asked if she could come in.

"Yeah, sure," I replied, minimising the window on my laptop so she would not see that I was chatting with Adrian.

"Tamara, can we talk?"

"About what, Mum? The fact that you have a tyrant for a husband and that he is as unreasonable as they get?"

"Now, Tamara."

"Don't, Mum," I interrupted. "Just don't. I have homework to do," I stated, turning away from her. I knew I was hurting her, but I didn't care. If she had tried to defend him, I would have been even more of a bitch. My mum left the room and I continued to chat with Adrian online and told him there was no possible way I could ever see him again. He said he would ride the tram home with me just to be with me. I forbade him as I knew my brother employed his little bratty friends as spies and was looking for any way to get back at me. I still didn't understand why he had such a personal vendetta against me. Prior to snitching about him getting his girlfriend pregnant, there was no memory of doing something to warrant such hatred.

CHAPTER 10

THE NEXT DAY AT SCHOOL, as soon as we went out to lunch, Fiona burst into tears because her father had found out about her relationship with Tony. He grounded her indefinitely and threatened to kill Tony if he tried to see her again. He actually got out his hammer and chased Tony down the street.

"I mean, seriously! How psycho can our fathers be?" Fiona stated.

"They really are living in the Stone Age," I replied. Mariam sat there, trying to be sympathetic to both our plights, but there wasn't much she could say. To try to lighten the mood, she reminded us that holidays were coming up.

"Yep, great! Even more alone time to think about how much my life sux!" I replied.

"There is no way I will be able to see Tony anymore without my dad finding out," Fiona added, dabbing at her eyes with a tissue.

"Shit. Can life get any more depressing?" I mumbled as we headed to class. I barely heard anything my teachers said that day, which became a regular trend. As I was sitting in maths class Friday pretending to do my work, I thought about how empty I felt. I kept looking at my watch; time seemed to be passing by in slow motion. I couldn't wait for the end of the school day, but then again, what did I have to look forward to? I would go home and read a book or watch DVDs on my own, and once again, I would lament my pointless existence. It was like nothing mattered anymore, and I was sinking deeper and deeper into this black hole of melancholy and despair. When the bell rang, I stayed in my seat and packed my things very slowly. My teacher asked me to close the door behind me and quickly left the room. Maybe she saw how miserable I was, but knew she couldn't do anything to help or simply didn't care. Did I even care about how unhappy I was? I buried my feelings away in that black hole. I walked home that afternoon and was almost run over by a car as I was in such a daze. The driver beeped at me, looking at me like I was crazy. I sat down on a bench at a nearby bus stop and took long, deep breaths. I almost just died. I knew I had to do something to snap out of this zombie state I was in.

By the time the September school holidays arrived, I had so much catching up to do. I spent the majority of the holidays at home writing and studying. I talked to Adrian online, but I knew I had to see him somehow. The last Saturday of the school holidays, I messaged Mariam and Fiona and told them we were going to Shadi's party. His parents were away for the weekend, and that was the perfect opportunity to be with our guys. Mariam messaged back that her guy didn't even know she existed, and she wanted to know how I was going to perform this miracle. I called her home number and asked her mum if Mariam could come over to help me study for our maths exam and possibly sleep over. Miraculously, she said yes. I almost squealed with excitement but had to stop myself in time so that my parents wouldn't hear me. I called Fi and demanded that she sneak out tonight and meet us at the shops near her house.

I was buzzing all day and couldn't wait to see Adrian. The way things ended with James made me realise even more that Adrian was the one. James was the other guy, the exciting one, the unattainable one, and that's why I thought I wanted him so badly. Anyway, he was a Uni student accustomed to having sex with the girls he dated. Here

I was, the freaking Virgin Mary, with my family dramas, begging him to please accept me as I was. Pfft! What was I thinking?

★ ★ ★

When my father opened the door and saw Mariam's sweet smile, he was lost for words. I informed him that she was going to help me study for our maths exam and then sleep over. Considering she was already at our house and the fact that I was failing mathematics, he really couldn't say no. We studied at the dining room table after dinner for two hours and then headed to bed. Once the clock struck eleven, we got changed, switched off the light in my room, and snuck out. We caught the tram to Fiona's and then caught a taxi to Shadi's house as we were running ridiculously late. The girls were scared shitless of getting caught, but I didn't care. I was sick of living by my father's laws, laws that were devoid of fairness and equality. My brother still went out every night, and Dad knew he was seeing Amelia. He was silent to Charlie's apparent disregard of his punishment. I remained a prisoner, serving my time with no chance of parole. I was going to see my boyfriend tonight.

We arrived at Shadi's just before twelve, and I introduced the girls to him and Sara.

"Where's Age?"

"Outside, near the pool," Sara answered. I rushed outside and straight into his arms. I kissed him so hard he had to pry me away.

"Whoa, Tam! Everyone is watching."

"And …" I replied, sliding my fingers through his hair and losing myself in his blue eyes. Mariam and Fiona walked up to us and I introduced Mariam to Adrian. I could read her well enough to know that she thought he was just as hot as I did. Tony finally arrived with his cousin Angelo. Angelo and Mariam hit it off instantly and made their way over to the esky. I raised my eyebrows at Mariam, and she grinned at me as she took a sip of her cruiser. I smiled back and turned to see Fiona and Tony already making out. I grabbed Adrian's hand and led him to a nearby sun chair. We couldn't keep our lips or hands off of one another. We soon remembered we were in public and pulled away from each other. I took his hand and led him upstairs. I knocked on a bedroom door, and after a long silence, we walked in. He sat on the bed, and I sat next to him; he instantly leaned over and passionately kissed me. He grabbed my shoulders and changed our positions so that I was lying on the bed with his body crushing mine. Adrian's touch was so gentle, and it made me want him even more. I removed my top as he stared at me quizzically. I kissed him hard and then pulled away to pull his top off.

"Tam, what are you doing?"

"Sshh," I interrupted, placing my finger on his lips. I grabbed his hand and placed it over my bra as he pulled me on top of him. As I felt his body mould to mine, I gasped but didn't pull away. Adrian removed my bra and kissed every part of my upper body. I shivered and dug my nails into his back. His breathing was as laboured as my own, and when I felt his hand caress the inside of my thigh, I pulled back to look into his eyes. Desire was written all over his face and reflected in his eyes.

"I want you so badly," I breathed into his ear.

"I want you even more," he replied as he licked the inside of my earlobe.

"I'm sorry, Age, but I don't think I can go any further," I said as I put my bra back on.

"I know," he replied with a sigh. "It's just … I mean … your skin is so fucking silky. I can't keep my hands off you." We had made out for so long that I felt like my lips were going to start bleeding.

"We better get back," Adrian stated as I nodded in agreement. As we walked out of the bedroom, I wondered how many kids were having sex in the other rooms and was glad I hadn't just lost my virginity at this party.

As soon as I walked outside, I noticed Mariam in the corner with Angelo experiencing her first kiss. I glanced over at the dancefloor and noticed Rania was here and dancing on her own. I could tell she was peaking.

"What's Rania on?" I asked Adrian.

"Probably Eckys or Ice."

"Age, where the hell did she get Eckys or Ice?"

"Probably from someone here. Tam, they're not that hard to get," he informed me as I raised my eyebrows. Rania was moving like she could actually feel every beat of the music. She was sensuously touching her body and smiling flirtatiously at this random guy in front of her. He eventually made his way over to her and pressed his body into hers. They continued to dance a bit too provocatively for my liking, and I turned away, totally embarrassed for her. After getting myself another breezer, I noticed Rania and the random guy on top of each other on the sun chair. I had to look away because I believed they were actually having sex. Shit, I knew I should do something. They probably weren't even using protection, but how the hell was I going to approach them. She better stop messing with her body and her life, or she was going to end up getting pregnant again (or even worse, contracting AIDS or something similar). Then I shrugged my shoulders and wondered why I should care when she despised me for no apparent reason.

A slow song came on, and I took Adrian by the hand and led him to the dance floor. He pushed my body closer towards him, and I closed my eyes, wishing this moment could last forever.

"I wish I could see you every day," I whispered in his ear.

"I know. I'm missing you, too," he replied as he kissed the side of my neck. When the song ended, we grabbed a few more drinks and joined our circle of friends.

"You fucking son of bitch! Didn't I warn you already to stay away from her?" I heard my cousin Rami yell out. I instantly pulled away from Adrian and turned towards the sound of his voice. He was storming towards us with his brother, Wael, behind him.

"Rami, what the fuck are you doing?" I stated, putting my hand on my cousin's chest. He slapped it away, snatched the cruiser out of my hand, and hurled it onto the floor.

"So you wanna get her drunk and drug fucked so you can take advantage of her, don't you, you little fucker? Take away her innocence?" He didn't wait for a response and instead lunged towards Adrian. Adrian dodged his blow and slammed his fist into Rami's face. I heard the impact of skin on bone, and seconds later, blood was streaming down Rami's nose. Rami hit Adrian's stomach, and he groaned and clutched at his right rib with his bleeding hand. I finally snapped out of my distressed trance and screamed for them to stop. Out of the corner of my eye, I saw Shadi bolting towards Rami, but Wael intervened, and they were soon beating each other up mercilessly. Sara heard the commotion and also tried to separate the boys to no avail. I was about to run for help when I saw Rami fall to the floor, his head hitting the side of the pool and then his whole body dropping like a dead weight straight into the water. Everyone stopped and turned towards the pool as Rami remained motionless.

"Fuck!" Adrian yelled as he jumped in and dragged Rami out of the pool with Wael's help. The back of his head was bleeding, but thankfully, he was breathing. I heard the sirens and was grateful someone had called an ambulance. We all stayed near Rami's side until the paramedics arrived. I looked over at Rania and noticed her smug smile. Had she told Rami we were here? Was she the one who had seen me in the city that day? Why did this bitch have it in for me?

I rode with my cousin in the ambulance, and the paramedics kept throwing questions at me. I ignored them and stroked Rami's hair. Even though he was a hot-tempered stupid Lebo and he had just broken my boyfriend's ribs, I wasn't angry enough at him to wish him hurt like this. I knew the repercussions of this night were going to be dreadful, and I prayed first for Rami to be OK and then for the ground to open up and swallow me whole.

I walked into the hospital like a zombie. Things kept happening around me, but I felt like a ghost: able to observe but not participate. I didn't want to be there. I couldn't stop the terrifying thoughts of what Dad would do to me once we got home. I was fucked! I couldn't breathe; I couldn't take this fear.

"Tam! Hello!"

"Yeah."

"Tamara, snap out of it!"

"What?" I almost yelled.

"Hey! You're weirding out! Let's go see Adrian and Shadi cause Rami is still in intensive care." I allowed Sara to drag me off the couch, but really wanted to tell her to fuck off. I was plotting and planning.

I rushed towards Adrian, plopped down on the hospital bed, and threw my arms around him. He groaned and clutched at his ribs.

"How badly are you hurt?" I asked him.

"Broken rib and a few bruises," he replied while trying to smile but then cringed in pain. I reached across and lightly caressed the bruise on his cheek and the cut on his lip. "I'm gonna go see Shadi," Sara informed me.

"I'll come, Sara. Age, I'll be right back," I told him as I lightly kissed him on his bruised cheek. Sara and I found Shadi asleep, and as we walked back towards Adrian's room, I asked her how bad Shadi was.

"Also has a broken rib and a broken nose," she replied, sighing. "I'll leave you guys alone and see how Rami is. By the way, Tam, Mum called, and I told her what happened. She should be here any minute with your mum and dad. I told her to try to calm your dad down before they got here."

"Yeah … OK … I'll just go jump off the roof now," I replied with a tired smile.

"Stay strong, munchkin," she whispered in my ear as she hugged me. When I walked back into Adrian's room, I found him dozing off. I tried not to make a sound, but he must have felt my presence as he opened his eyes and smiled warmly at me.

"Come here, Tam." As I lay on the bed next to him, he stroked my hair. "You OK?"

"I should be the one looking after you."

"These are just physical injuries. They'll heal. You, on the other hand, are going through some real emotional shit. What are you gonna tell your dad when he gets here?"

"Um … probably catch ya later and then I'll run the other way." He smiled and kissed me softly. We sat there in silence with Adrian stroking my palm with his thumb. I squeezed his hand and stood up when Sara appeared in the doorway.

"Let's go wait in Rami's room, Tam." I nodded and smiled down at Adrian.

"I wish I could be beside you when you confront him," Adrian said me as he stared intensely into my eyes.

"Are you crazy? Dad would shoot you if he could get his hands on a gun! Age, we have to end this!"

"Tam, chillax. We'll talk about this later."

"I hate it when you tell me to chillax! I can't keep doing this; it's just too much drama."

"You just don't want to stand up to your dad and tell him you want to be with me! You're embarrassed of me, aren't you?"

"Yes, I am! Is that what you want to hear? You are insignificant and no longer mean anything to me!"

"Where is this coming from, Tamara?"

"God, why I would choose to be with this boy instead of a man like James is beyond me!" *What are you doing? I can't keep hurting him like this.*

"What the fuck are you talking about, Tam? Who is James?"

"Wouldn't you like to know? Just forget it. It's over, Adrian!"

"Are you on something? Who are you?" *Yeah, who are you? Shut up! I need to do this. It is killing me, but it must be done.*

"The real me. The person I was while I was with you wasn't the real me. Sorry," I replied as I shrugged my shoulders indifferently.

"Tam," he began looking at me like I was already in a straightjacket with drool running down my chin.

"Adrian," I interrupted, looking at him with fire in my eyes. "You liked a shy, gutless, selfish girl. Let go of the person you thought I was and move on to some bimbo who won't drain your life and cause you to get beaten up every other day."

"Hurry up, Tam. Your dad is gonna be here any minute," Sara said. I had forgotten she was still there.

"Chill, Sara."

"What the fuck is wrong with you?" she asked as we walked away from Adrian's room. "Why are you so … so nasty all of a sudden? Why the fuck did you say all that to Adrian? How could you hurt him like that? Who's this James?"

"You are the last person I have to explain myself to," I replied as we walked into Rami's hospital room. We found him awake, but he wouldn't even look at me. I just stood by the door, occasionally glancing over at him. Wael walked in a few minutes after we arrived with his hand plastered. He had smashed his knuckles open, and his face was as bruised as the rest of the boys'. Lydia rushed past me and straight towards Rami. She put her hand under his chin and moved his face towards the light. She looked at him with anger emanating from her eyes and stated quietly that he was a stupid boy. He gasped at her and opened his mouth to speak, but she pointed her finger at him, silently demanding he not say a word.

I then turned towards the sound of Mum's voice. Mum was whispering to Dad that he needed to calm down, but he was purposely ignoring her. Charlie was trailing behind them. I couldn't meet Dad's eyes as he walked in. I stared at Mum, but she wouldn't meet my eyes as all three of them filled the room. Wael walked towards me to leave, but Dad stopped him by placing his hand on his shoulder.

'Rami … Wael. What you did tonight was not needed," my father began sternly in Arabic. "When you get to my age, you will realise that violence does not solve anything. Your father, my brother, and I learned that years ago. I appreciate you looking out for your younger cousin, and I agree that Tamara should not be seeing this boy, but putting him in hospital makes us no better than him. I don't want you to ever go near this boy again, understood?" They both nodded, and Dad walked away quickly. He motioned for Mum to follow him, and she signalled for Charlie and me to follow her. I wondered what was in store for me when we got home.

'Where are your parents boys?' My father asked before leaving.

'Outside, dad is having a cigarette and mum is calming him down.' Wael replied.

'I will call him when I get home,' my father said while walking out the door.

We walked to the car in silence, and on the way home, the eerie quiet continued. Maybe Dad was waiting for me to say something while I was waiting for him to go totally mental on me.

As we walked into the living room, Dad finally spoke, "Tamara, once again, you disobeyed me and lied to me! Who have you become? Who is this girl dressed like a doll standing in front of me? Your actions tonight put your cousins in hospital. When I came to check on you and Mariam and found your room empty, I called your cousin Rami to bring you home, but God knows what you were doing with that boy to have caused such a violent outburst."

"Nothing!" I interrupted. "My actions tonight were nowhere near as bad as your son's, and yet you give us the same punishment and then expect me to go back to being your dutiful daughter!"

"*Ya sharmota*, you slut," he boomed as his slapped me across the face. My cheek instantly burned up, and my left eye felt like it was going to explode. Tears ran down my face as I stared at him with as much anger as I could muster.

"I detest you!" I spat the words at him, "and if you don't know what that means, look it up in the fucking dictionary!" I yelled and then bolted to my room. I hauled the desk in front of the door as I wasn't allowed a lock on my bedroom door. I waited for the sound of his heavy footsteps, but the house remained quiet. I sat down on the floor with my back leaning on my bed and stared at my bedroom door. I would never allow myself to cry over my fucked-up family! I just continued to sit there, numb. I wished I had telekinetic abilities so I could cause something to fall on him. I wanted to hit him with something. I took deep breaths and willed myself to stop crying. I fell asleep sitting up and woke up in the middle of the night just long enough to crawl into bed.

CHAPTER 11

THE FOLLOWING MORNING, AFTER A fretful night's sleep, I stayed in bed for as long as possible. I then turned on my computer and overloaded my diary with extremely depressing thoughts and feelings. My stomach kept growling, and I ignored its hunger pains. I could hear my mum in the kitchen, but I couldn't hear anyone else in the house. Sara hopped on Facebook chat and asked if I was OK.

"What do u mean?"

"U totally freaked out at da hospital last nite!"

"Yeah …"

"Tam, seriously what da fuck is wrong with u?"

"Sara, I can't talk about this now."

"U said some real hurtful things 2 Adrian and mentioned a guy called James before u broke up with him! You were a cold and nasty bitch!"

I didn't know what to reply. "Sara, I got 2 go toilet. Bye."

I quickly signed off and put my head in my hands. I couldn't tell her the truth because she would just go straight to Adrian and tell him everything. This was for the best; he couldn't keep getting hurt because of me. *Although you are protecting him, you are also breaking your own heart. I know!*

After I had calmed down, I called Sara and asked her about how Shadi and Adrian were doing. I wanted to tell her everything. I felt like I was being pulled in two different directions, and I didn't want to decide which path to take. Sara said Shadi and Adrian were getting out of hospital today, but Rami had to stay another night. Sara then informed me that Rania had called her and asked what had happened last night. The poor girl didn't remember a thing, and when Sara mentioned she was screwing a random in front of everyone, she burst into tears and hung up the phone.

No matter how curious I was, I vowed to never to pop a pill. Before ending the conversation, Sara asked me if anything happened with Adrian and me at the party and if that had to do with me breaking up with him. I told her that I wasn't ready to sleep with him just yet and asked if she had spoken to him, taking the attention away from my actions last night. She replied that she hadn't and asked whether I had tried to speak to him. I said I would try later. It was enough to appease her, but I knew she would eventually want to know my reasons. All I wanted to do was run away from all this drama and heartache.

I couldn't ignore my hunger pains any longer and popped my head into the kitchen. I found Mum sitting by the kitchen bench, smoking a cigarette and staring off into space.

"Hi, Mum."

"Hi, Tamara," she replied as she turned towards me with a warm smile.

"Where's Dad?"

"At Uncle Alfred's."

"Did you speak to him today?"

"No."

"What happens now?"

"No idea, but we must give your father time to calm down," she replied in Arabic, proof that she was agitated.

"Give *him* time to calm down? How dare he hit me! I'm not a little child anymore!"

"Tamara, now calm down. You know he didn't mean it."

"Bullshit! Why do you always defend him? You don't even love each other anymore! You think I don't see it?" She didn't reply, but only stared off into space once again. When the tears began streaming down her face, I walked over and patted her arm.

"I'm sorry, Mum. I can be such a little bitch. I didn't mean it."

"It's OK, *habibi*," she whispered and then proceeded to make me breakfast.

"Mum, why are you so patient with him?"

"It long story. Tell you different time." I didn't bother correcting her and we ate in silence. After doing the dishes, I went back into my sanctuary. I began to write my father a letter. I tried to explain what it felt like growing up in this family with his strict rules. How all I wanted was to experience everything other teenage girls did.

I sighed and scrunched up the paper. I knew what his response would be. "You are not like every other teenager, Tamara. You come from a respectable Lebanese Catholic family. You are not some *Australiye* roaming the street and doing what you damn want. Under my roof, you will obey my rules." Blah … blah … blah! I had heard it so many times before; it was just so predictable. *Don't know why you even bother! He will never understand where you are coming from because he has no soul and no heart.*

I left my room to have a late lunch and was thankful Dad was still not home. I heard him come in just before dinner time, and I quickly turned off the light in my room. I lay there in the dark for hours, thinking of all the different paths my life could take. All of them were dreary and terrifying. Nothing was in my control, and more than anything, I wished I had the courage to storm out that door and never return.

CHAPTER 12

THE FIRST DAY BACK AT school, we once again sat in our miserable circle. This was going to be a long and dreary term.

"I'm sorry, besties; I got you girls into so much trouble."

"It's OK, Tam. It was worth it for me," Fiona replied with a sad smile.

"And for me," Mariam added, "but my mum adamantly swore that she would disown me if I remained friends with you."

"I knew she'd hate me! Your dad must, too, yeah, Fi?"

"Nah, I told him I went to the party alone, and you girls met me there. But Mi Mi and I had to call our parents after you left for the hospital because the cops wouldn't let us go without a parent present. Thank God Tony had left before dad got there. That would have been a total disaster," Fiona said as she looked sadly at the picture of her and Tony on her phone.

"Was Angelo a good kisser, Mi Mi?" I asked, trying to lighten the mood.

"Well, I think so. I mean I haven't kissed anyone before him, obviously, but he wasn't all slobbery so I guess, yeah"

"Fi will you risk being seen with Tony again?"

"Duh! I mean who else do I wanna jump every time I see him?" she replied dramatically. Mariam and I laughed along with her.

"I'm glad I have you girls to keep me sane," I told them as I hugged each of them.

"And if it wasn't for you, Tam, we would never have experienced our first kisses," Fiona replied.

"Anyway," I sighed as I heard the bell ring, "let's try to get to class on time. We don't need another reason for our parents to skitz it at us." As I walked into class, I smiled at our English teacher, Miss Mitchell. She was strict, but really understanding and an amazing teacher. Today, we were beginning our essays on *Romeo and Juliet,* and she suggested that we try to come up with our own essay question.

"Can't we just choose one of these?" Fiona asked, holding up the list of essay questions Miss Mitchell had given us.

"Yes, of course, Fiona, but for those of you who wish to explore a different avenue, have a go at constructing your own essay question." She left us to work individually. After about ten minutes, I crossed out a few sentences, rewrote them, and walked towards her desk.

"Miss Mitchell, can I go over this with you?"

"Certainly, Tamara," she replied, pulling a chair closer to hers. I sat down and passed her my notebook.

"Tamara, this is very impressive. Explain to me how you are going to explore this question. What will your main argument be?"

"Well, um … basically that if Romeo and Juliet's love wasn't forbidden, it wouldn't have been as strong."

"OK. Convince me of this. Elaborate."

"Well, if you tell a teenager she can't be with a particular person, it makes her want that person even more. I mean, that's just a fact. It's similar to reverse psychology really, except that it is the opposite. You know what I mean, right?" I paused, and she nodded with an amused expression on her face. "Anyway, I think that Romeo and Juliet's love wouldn't have been so tragic or as heart-rending if their families weren't enemies, and that's pretty obvious. But the fact that their love was forbidden and caused so much conflict and violence around them made them hold on to each other even more and made the goodness of their love shine that much brighter."

"Excellent, Tamara. Well done. Now use quotes, develop this argument, and dazzle me with your insight."

"Sure," I replied, smiling shyly. "Thanks, Miss Mitchell." I walked away still smiling, and I suddenly heard someone snicker. My eyes met Rania's, and from the look on her face, it was obvious that she wasn't happy with the praise I had just received.

"Rania, I need to speak to you please," Miss Mitchell called out. Rania mumbled something under her breath and made her way over to Miss Mitchell's desk. They spoke in low tones, but I did manage to hear the word *fail* come from Miss Mitchell's mouth. Rania looked devastated as she sat back down at her desk. I watched her for a few minutes as she stared blankly at the paper in front of her. My thoughts wandered away from her as I considered bringing my story in to show Miss Mitchell. I thought she would probably be thrilled that I had won the competition since she had always encouraged me with my writing. I opened my notebook, reread my essay question, and laughed under my breath.

On my way home from school, I saw Rania sitting on her own in the park and smoking a cigarette. I walked over to her and asked if I could bum one. She looked at me incredulously, took one out of her packet, and handed it to me. I placed it in my mouth and leaned over as she lit it for me.

"Listen, I know we are like so not friends, but I heard about Wissam's party this Saturday, and I wanna go. Since you will be the only person there I know, I thought we could go together," I stated and then took a long drag of my dart.

"Are you messing with me?"

"Huh?"

"Seriously, Tamara. Go find someone else to play your mind games with!"

"I'm not playing games, Rania. I am sick of being this. I wanna live it up, and you are the perfect person to live it up with." She continued to stare at me in disbelief. "Give me your phone." I typed in my number. "I'll meet you there at seven. If there are any issues, call me." I handed her phone back and walked away. I flicked my ciggy away and smiled as I glanced back at her. She was looking at me like I were an alien or some foreign being. *The irony of it was that you are. Aren't you sick of being the perfect little Lebanese girl? I couldn't believe I had just done that, but I knew I had to take control of my life somehow.*

CHAPTER 13

That first week of school couldn't have possibly gone any slower, and my thoughts were consumed by memories of Adrian and me. We hadn't spoken since the hospital, and I knew it was for the best. But more than anything, I longed to be in his arms, and I lamented my cursed life.

★ ★ ★

Saturday morning, I woke up feeling the worst I have ever felt. I was drowning in my melancholy, and I felt like I was losing control of everything in my life. I placed my head back down on my pillow and stared at the ceiling. I couldn't believe I still had Rob Patz's poster still up there. What a loser! I remembered how I used to dream and fantasise about him a few years ago. I daydreamed about Adrian and began to cry. Why was life so much easier for others and a constant battle for me? Why? I wanted to disappear from reality, and normally, my fantasies allowed me that momentary escape, but it wasn't working this time. I started sobbing into my pillow and wished I could just sleep this day away.

I eventually signed onto Facebook and started chatting with Fiona and Mariam. They asked if they could come over for a DVD night. I replied that I had plans with Rania. They both told me to quit messing around. I replied that I was going to Wissam's party to have some fun, which was seriously lacking in our lives. Fiona asked if something had happened that was making me act crazy. Mariam asked bluntly what the hell was wrong with me and why I was suddenly such a bitch. I ignored them both and signed off. I could not justify wasting another moment of this day on being the old me!

For most of the day, I stayed out of my family's way and said that I was going to bed early. I picked the sexiest clothing that I owned, a short skirt that barely covered my ass and a low-cut top. I put on stiletto shoes that I had abandoned months ago when my father forbade me to wear them. I curled my hair, put on heavy make-up, and stashed a condom, which I stole from Charlie's room, in my handbag before I left. Why I took the condom I did not know. *You want to use it. That's why. No, it is for Rania. Don't want her to be in the same situation again. Yep, keep telling yourself that! Arghhh, I am losing my mind! Who am I?*

Sara called me as I was on the tram and asked if I wanted her to try to talk to Adrian.

"What's the point?"

"OK, Tam. You're acting weird again!"

"I'm on my way to Wissam's party, and the last person I want to think about is Adrian."

"Tam, why the fuck are you going to Wissam's party?"

"Uh, to have fun. To get high and finally lose my virginity."

"Ah, seriously, babe. This isn't funny anymore."

"I don't give a fuck what you think," I replied and hung up the phone. She tried to call back instantly, and I rejected her call and turned off the phone. *Did you really just talk to her like that? Maybe this person I am becoming isn't so bad after all.*

As soon as I arrived at Wissam's house, I saw Rania waiting out the front. She smiled at me and handed me a dart.

"I still can't believe you came. Whatever you are on, I want some."

"Not on anything, babe, but I want to be," I replied with a devilish smile. She handed me a small pill engraved with a love heart.

"Here's to an awesome night," Rania said as she swallowed hers without water. I did the same. I knew I was being totally reckless, but at that moment, I really didn't care. We walked inside and heard a few wolf whistles on our way to the backyard. I checked out the guys and admitted none were as gorgeous as Adrian. We said hi to Wissam as he handed us a cruiser each. I gulped mine down in fifteen minutes, while Rania was already on her third. I started feeling the effect of the drug, as well as the alcohol. It felt fucking amazing! I made my way to the dance floor and started dancing with Rania. A hot guy with a tight grey t-shirt and a tattoo of a cross on his forearm made his way over to us. He grabbed my hand and brought my body closer to his. I looked at Rania who was smiling absently as she glanced over at Wissam who was pashing some skank. She popped another pill and then grabbed a nearby guy by the hand and led him into the house.

I continued to dance and flirt outrageously with my hottie until he made a grab for my ass. I let him, and we started pashing. He took my hand and led me into a bedroom. God, his biceps felt good under my fingertips! He threw me down on the bed and took his top off. He climbed over me and began to kiss me while pushing down my skirt. He moved aside so I could take his jeans off. He then grabbed my head and pushed it down, and as I was about to pull down his jocks, I turned aside and threw up all over the lovely beige carpet. He made a disgusted noise and walked out of the room with his clothes in his arms. I moaned and tried to sit up. I managed to make it to the bathroom and threw up again in the sink. I looked at myself in the mirror, and all I could think about was how good it would have felt if my father had found me in that compromising position. I could just imagine the look on his face! His sweet, innocent daughter, half naked, about to give a guy a …; I had truly fucked up that opportunity. I remembered the look on Dad's face when he caught me taking twenty bucks from his wallet two years ago. He demanded to know what I was going to use the money for. I couldn't help myself: I lied and said ciggies. His face turned such a deep shade of red that I really thought his eyeballs were going to pop right out of his face. He slapped me across the face, twice that time, on each cheek. I just stared at him and said, "Well, one of your kids had to take after your wife!" He slapped me again and sent me to my room for the rest of the day. That was one of the rare times when I had openly defied and tested him to see what he would do. I needed the money for make-up, which I wasn't allowed to wear, but that was the last time I tested the waters until recently. *But fuck, did he deserve to be disobeyed! His cold heart needed to be ripped apart.*

I came back to the present, and after I washed my face and felt like I could take two steps without falling over, I sent Rania a text and told her I was leaving. I waited five minutes and went to look for her. I found her passed out on the cold tiles in the en suite of the main bedroom. I leaned over her and shook her. She remained unconscious. God, this girl was annoying! I lifted her head and placed it on my lap as I sat down.

"Rania, come on. Wake up! I want to go home!" Still no response.

"Fucking wake up!" I yelled in her ear. "It's your funeral if your dad finds you here tomorrow morning!" I continued to shake her, and my eyes really focused on her face. No! No fucking way! I put my ear close to her mouth and couldn't hear or feel anything. I felt for a pulse but realised I was still too drunk and couldn't concentrate long enough to feel anything. I put my ear on her chest and still nothing! *Oh my God! She isn't! She just can't be!* I called the ambulance and said a girl was passed out and didn't look like she's breathing. I gave them the address and hung up before they could ask any questions. I pulled her hair away from her face and stroked her forehead. Was she colder? Was she really dead? I stood up and left. I ran out and yelled out to Wissam that Rania was passed out upstairs, and he should get to her *now*! I ran and ran and let the cold wind whip at my face. I stopped at a park and sat on the swing, feeling numb and unable to think clearly. Which suburb was I in? I was never going to be me again. I … was it my … I mean … it was partly my fault Rania died tonight. God, I couldn't … I just couldn't think about it!

Tears of confusion, worry, shame, and pure rage were running down my cheeks. What had I done? Being this other person could have taken a life away. I scrutinised a barren tree and wondered why it was so lifeless. It was standing alone as the other flourishing trees were placed metres away from it. I felt sorry for it, as it was probably feeling as isolated and in despair as I was.

I found my phone in my hand and dialled Adrian's number. No answer. I dialled him again and still no answer. On the second ring of my third call, I heard his mumbled, half-asleep voice.

"Hello."

"Age, I know you don't want to ever speak to me again," I sobbed into the phone, "but I really need you to come get me."

"What's wrong? Where are you?" he asked, now wide awake.

"I don't know. Some park."

"How can you not know, Tam?"

"I ran here. I just need you to come get me, please. Please something bad happened. Something so bad!" I sobbed and spluttered my words.

"Tam, calm down!" he interrupted again. "Go to the nearest intersection, and tell me where you are. Try to find something familiar!"

"OK, give me a minute," I replied as I walked towards the street signs. "I'm on the corner of Rathdowne and Newry streets."

"I'll be there in ten minutes. Do not go anywhere else!"

"I won't," I replied before hanging up the phone. I waited on the swing, pushing my legs away from the ground, wishing I could fly off this thing and away from my life. I closed my eyes and concentrated on the blackness. *Just think about the blackness*, I kept repeating to myself until I heard a car engine. My eyes quickly opened and I saw Adrian bolting towards me. I stood up and flew into his arms.

"Shhh," he whispered softly into my ear as I sobbed on his shoulder. He led me towards the car, placed me in the back seat, and cranked up the heater. I noticed a guy in trackies walking away from the car.

"Who's that?"

"My brother."

'Where's he going?'

"He's just giving us some privacy," Adrian replied as he tucked my hair behind my ears.

"Age, I'm so, so sorry," I began looking deep into his eyes.

"It's OK. Don't worry now. We just need to get you back home and sort this out tomorrow. What happened?" he asked as his eyes moved from my face all the way down to my toes.

"Can we talk about it tomorrow, please?" He sighed and looked away. We drove to my house mostly in silence, aside from the directions I gave them. I asked Adrian's brother to park a street away. I thanked him and stepped out of the car. Adrian did the same and took my hand.

"Are you going to be OK?"

"Ah, yeah … I'll be OK," I replied, not wanting to meet his eyes as I knew I would burst into tears if I did.

"I'll call you tomorrow, OK?"

"OK," I mumbled as I turned and swiftly walked away from him before he could see me crying. I snuck into my room, tore off my clothes and shoes, and hid them in the back of my closet. I was exhausted. As my head hit the pillow, I cried myself to sleep.

CHAPTER 14

I WOKE UP WITH THE worst headache and the puffiest eyes ever. I walked into the kitchen in a haze and found my mother in her usual spot with a cigarette in one hand and a cup of coffee in the other.

"Morning, Mum."

"Tamara, sit down. We need to talk."

"OK," I replied. "What's wrong?"

"So many things," she paused and stared intently into her coffee cup. If it were Arabic coffee, I would have sworn she were trying to read her future, but it was just Nescafe Gold. She remained lost in her thoughts until I cleared my throat.

"Tamara, did I tell you about my life before I meet your father?"

"Yeah. You told me how you were so wild and beautiful," I replied as I put some bread in the toaster.

"I'll make you breakfast. Sit." She fussed around for a while before turning back towards me. I had never seen my mother so frazzled before.

"Well, because I was so wild, I never thought about getting married. So many men came to the house. Mostly my father's students. They hear how beautiful his daughters are." She informed me while passing me two pieces of toast.

"Heard, Mum. It's in the past, and I still can't believe *jedo, grandpa*, was a French professor. You must have been so proud to have a father who was so educated."

"I know you judge your father for just being a restaurant owner, Tamara. He is very smart, but his father have no money to pay to keep him in school, and that's why he stop. Not because he not smart. OK, so I try to say that many men ask for my hand, but none good enough. I was too—how do you say in English *shefe hele?*"

"Conceited," I replied, smothering my toast with peanut butter.

"Yes, OK. One of things my father hated. There was one man I still think about."

"Really?" I stated with a raised eyebrow before taking a bite of my toast.

"He was half French, half Lebanese. My father knew his father when he was little. One day, they come and see us."

"*Visit* is a better word to use, Mum."

"OK, *visit*, Miss Smart! This six months before I meet your father. This man, his name Andre. He so beautiful and very tall and has dark hair and green eyes. His eyelashes as long as yours. Very smart. He was working for an international company."

"As what?" I asked.

"I no remember. Anyway, he told my father five minutes after he saw me that he love me and want to marry me. When my father told me of this, I laughed and laughed. How could he love me after five minutes, I told my father. What a *habele*, an idiot. My father got angry as he hated it when I judged people too much, too quickly."

"*Harshly*, Mum."

"Alright, too harsshy" I smiled and let her go on.

"My father told me think about this because he like him and respect him. I told him to leave me alone because I don't want to marry anyone; I want to be free all my life. I was too wild. I don't know where I got it from. My mother was an angel, so quiet and obedient. Andre stopped coming to see us, and six months later I meet your father."

"Mum, you never told me why you thought Dad was the one."

"*Ya bente*, my daughter. He was not my one, he was at first but not always."

"Mum, are you serious?" I asked, staring at her incredulously.

"I explain. Wait," she paused and stared into her coffee cup. She stood up, poured herself some more, sat back down, and lit a cigarette.

"Mum, you OK?"

"Yes, yes. Your father came along, and he had money and lived in Australia. Back then, living in another country was a Godsend. Well, my father liked him, and he kept pushing and pushing. I don't think anything special your father had, but I promised I would think about him. Then my father got sick, and your father was in Lebanon on holiday, no work so he came to see us every day. Linda, your oldest auntie, started pushing, too."

"Why?' I asked. "Why were they trying to control your freaking life?"

"Tamara, calm down. *Jedic*, your grandfather, was dying. He knew it was soon, and he wanted us with husbands who would buy food and support us when he died. This killed him quickly I think, this worry. He pushed me and my sisters to marry to the men who love us. We have no choice and I did love him at first," she paused and sighed. I placed my hand over hers, wanting to hug her, but Mum and I weren't like that.

"Your father had money and his own business in Australia, so I married him, and we come here. He not tell me they all lived together, his family. I hated it! I hated his family. Living with them, hell. *Setic*, your grandmother, was mean, very mean and jealous. All of them jealous because I beautiful and full of life and because your father and I in love and touch and talk. I cook and clean for all of them, like a slave," my mother revealed, slamming her fist onto the table.

"Mum …" I didn't know what to say, but I just wanted to comfort her somehow. She had never confided in me like this before.

"They crushed us, Tamara."

"What do you mean, Mum?"

"They cause trouble, and we fight. I try to show him it was not me but all of them, but they play with his mind. They lie and say, 'Your wife lazy.' I got very angry two times, and your father hit me. I never forgive him or his family for this. They are miserable people and their fault your father and me like strangers and soon we never show love. You understand now why we like this?" she asked me, looking deep into my eyes. I saw the tears swimming in hers, threatening to overflow, but they didn't. She swallowed, and they disappeared. I wondered how she was able to do that, to swallow her grief away. It was probably through years of practice.

"I'm so sorry, Mum," I replied, standing up and putting my arms around her. She held me tightly and then pushed me away.

"Sit down, Tamara, I have more. I wanted to go to school and learn English and do a course, do something, but again, his family always saying no. They are nothing, and I had to be nothing."

"Now I know why you hate going over to *teta*, grandma, and *jedo's*, grandpa's," I said while I put the dishes into the dishwasher.

"Yes, and why I always angry at your father's brothers. If only we stayed in Lebanon, everything would be different."

"So sorry again, mum."

"Tamara, I do not want you go through the same. I want you to be happy and strong. You have to argue and show your father you know what is right, too." She looked me straight in the eyes and continued, "I want you to be free! To love and enjoy life, OK?"

"OK, Mum," I replied, trying not to cry.

"You are special, *ya bente*," she whispered, wiping tears off my cheeks. "Now, you are going to see this boy. What his name?"

"Adrian."

"Yes, you see him, and be home before your dad come home."

"What, are you serious?"

"Yes, I see he make you happy. Now go get ready, and I will take you." She leaned over this time and held me close. I squealed in her ear and ran to my room. I couldn't believe my mother was going to help me see Adrian behind my dad's back. Knowing all this changed everything.

★ ★ ★

Mum dropped me off at the park near Adrian's house. I had texted him and asked if I could come over. He responded by saying that we should meet at the park and talk beforehand.

"Hey," I said as I walked towards him.

"Hey," he replied as I sat beside him on the bench. "How are you feeling?"

"Really hung-over."

"Tam, you need to tell me what happened."

"I know, but I was hoping we could deal with it together," I replied, placing my hand in his.

"I …" he began while standing up. He walked a few steps away and paced back while running his fingers through his hair. "Tam, you said some really … well, bitchy things at the hospital."

"I know, but I didn't want you to get hurt anymore; please, Age, you have to believe me!" I cried, getting up and walking towards him. I grabbed his shoulders and turned him towards me.

"How do I know that is not how you really feel?"

"Uh Age I…"

"You said that I was a child and you wanted to be with a man. You wanted to be with some guy named James."

"Fuck, I didn't mean any of that!" I muttered under my breath.

"Who is James, Tam?"

"Ah," I began turning away from him, as I didn't want to see the hurt on his face when I answered his question, "James is this guy I met at Melbourne University."

"Why were you at Melbourne Uni?"

"I was just exploring, and anyway, he invited me to his dorm party, and I went. And I don't know why, Age. It was after we had that fight on Facebook chat, and I was angry at everything. We kissed; that's all. And then I ended it," I turned to face him. "I ended it cause I love you, Age. I chose you!" I tried to pull him close, but he pushed me away.

"And that is meant to make it all OK!? You fucking cheated on me, Tam."

"I'm sorry. I was just wanting to rebel in all the ways I could."

"You mean you wanted to string two guys along, right?" he replied looking at me with such anger and disappointment that I had to look away. "Tam, how can I trust you not to do that again?" I couldn't answer him, and I couldn't turn around. I didn't want him to see me cry. He grabbed my shoulders and turned me towards him. His face broke down a little when he saw my face. The anger in his eyes disappeared and a bit of softness replaced it.

"Age, I really am sorry. I don't know what is going on with me. James was my worst mistake, and I know you won't be able to trust me again, but I will always love you," I told him as I stroked his face and turned to walk away.

"Where are you going?"

"Home," I replied turning back towards him.

"You can't. I already told my mum you are coming over for lunch."

"So you wanted me to stay either way?"

"I hate it when you do that."

"Do what?"

"When you look up at me with those beautiful eyes. You make all my anger disappear!"

"I just want us to go back to the way we were."

"I can't promise that will happen, but we can try," he said as he put his arms around my waist. I stood up on the tips of my sneakers and kissed him. As we headed to his house, I started biting my nails.

"What's wrong?"

"I'm nervous."

"Too late now. My mum's cooked up a feast for lunch, so you can't bail."

"I know," I replied as I trudged along beside him. His house was old-school but immaculate. "Hi, Mrs Fontana," I said shyly as Adrian and I walked into the kitchen.

"Please call me Patricia," she replied, giving me a warm hug. I looked around, and the kitchen was warm and inviting. The aromas overwhelmed my senses, and my stomach began to grumble.

"That smells wonderful, Mrs Fontana. I mean Patricia," I stated, moving closer to where she stood near the stove.

"I hope you like Italian sausages, and I'm also making spaghetti with my famous meatballs," she informed me as she stirred the pot of sauce.

"Mmm, sounds delicious, but you shouldn't have gone to all this trouble."

"Don't be silly, Tamara. We have a feast like this every Sunday. After all, we are wogs," she said with a warm smile. Adrian had inherited his mother's startling blue eyes and her Italian nose. His mother must have been even more beautiful when she was younger. She didn't have the same petite features as my mum, but she had striking looks. She handed me a glass of Coke as Adrian's father walked in.

"This must be Tamara," he said shaking my hand. "Nice to meet you."

"And you, Mr Fontana," I replied. Before I could say anything else, he walked away. Adrian had gotten his curly hair and height from his father.

"Mum, I'm gonna give Tamara a tour of the house," Adrian said as he grabbed a roll off the platter.

"Yes, yes, go," she replied as she slapped his hand, but Adrian held onto the roll and stuffed it all into his mouth.

"My son is a pig. Sorry, Tamara," Mrs Fontana muttered and shrugged her shoulders while I giggled.

"Let's go to your room," I whispered to Adrian as I turned away from his mother. He led me through a long corridor to the last room on the right. When I stepped into his bedroom, my eyes absorbed everything: his trophies, photos, and strewn dirty laundry, which he quickly kicked under his bed.

"I didn't know you were this good at soccer," I said as I picked up one of his many trophies.

"I'm OK," he replied with a shrug.

"Gorgeous, smart, and modest: What more can I ask for in a boyfriend. I mean, not to say that we are back to being exclusive. Shit."

"It's OK, Tam," he interrupted. "It's OK."

"Can I see you play one day?" I asked him as I caressed his cheek.

"Yeah, when my team makes the finals, which will be never!"

"Are you embarrassed or worried about introducing me to your soccer mates?" I asked with a frown.

"I'm worried they will embarrass me because as soon as they see how freaking hot you are, they will sleaze all over you and act like dickheads."

"Are they that bad?" I asked, chuckling.

"Yeah they are," he said.

"Did you ever dream of being an international soccer player?" I asked him, looking at all his trophies and medals.

"Yeah, but then dad droned into me that it wasn't a career, and anyway, I wanna be a lawyer now. I'm doing year eleven legal this year, and I'm killing it."

"I didn't know that," I muttered. "There is so much more to know about each other."

"Yeah, like why your mum is suddenly cool about us," he said as he plopped down on his bed.

"I'll tell you all about it later," I began as I sat on his lap, my legs on either side of his. "She really opened up to me today," I said, running my fingers through his thick hair. Our lips met, and as our kisses became passionate, we heard his mum call us for lunch, and we pulled away from one another, both embarrassed as if she was right there standing over us. He showed me the rest of his house and at least our parents had one thing in common; their taste in furniture. I met Adrian's sister just before we sat down for lunch, and her and his brother were as warm and friendly as their mum. We ate in awkward silence until Andrew, Adrian's brother, started talking about how busy his work was and how they were all working overtime to get the cars serviced in time.

"It is good to keep busy. Do you agree, Tamara?" Mr Fontana asked me.

"Definitely," I replied, nodding my head.

"What are your future study plans, dear?" Mrs Fontana asked.

"I am hoping to complete a degree in psychology and arts."

"That is very impressive. You have a smart one there, son," Mr Fontana said, nodding his head towards me.

"I know," Adrian replied, beaming at me.

"So you plan to be a psychologist then?" his father asked me.

"Yes," I replied, tongue-tied all of a sudden.

"Tamara, also wants to be a writer, Dad; she just won a writing competition."

"Well done. But writing will only be a hobby, of course."

"Of course," I answered, squeezing Adrian's hand before he said anything. How funny it is how all wog fathers think the same.

"Angela wants to be a doctor," Mr Fontana stated.

"Actually, darling, she wants to be a vet," Mrs Fontana informed him.

"Yeah, Dad. I mean how awesome would it be healing little puppies every day," Angela said with dreamy eyes. Her father rolled his, but luckily she hadn't seen him. Adrian frowned towards his father but kept his mouth shut. I could tell he really wanted to say something.

"Why don't you kids go sit outside while I make some coffee," Mrs Fontana said as she began to clear the table.

"I'll help you with the dishes, Mrs Fontana ah I mean Patricia."

"No, dear, you will not. You are a guest in this house, so go and sit," she shooed us away and continued cleaning up.

As we headed to the living room, Angela and I started discussing what our favourite shows were. Soon we were gushing over the hottest male leads and how Greys Anatomy was still the greatest show ever, even though it was in its tenth season. Adrian and Andrew had escaped to play Wii. When it came time for me to leave, Mrs Fontana and Angela hugged me goodbye. I was relieved the lunch had gone well. Andrew dropped me off a few blocks away from home. He turned his face away as Adrian gave me a kiss goodbye. Adrian whispered in my ear that he would call me tonight, and I just nodded and smiled. My cheeks ached from smiling so much. I tried to remember another time in my life when I had been this happy, and I couldn't.

CHAPTER 15

When I saw Dad's car in the driveway, I felt my heart drop to the ground. I wondered why Mum hadn't called to warn me. I opened the door and headed towards the living room. The volume was immediately muted on the television. As my eyes turned towards my mother, I noticed her bruised cheek instantly. I looked at my father, and his eyes were ready to pop out of his head.

"How dare you defy me once again?" he roared. I was afraid he was actually going to have a heart attack as his neck muscles were bulging.

"Joseph, calm down," my mother whispered in Arabic. She wouldn't dare speak to him in English as it would infuriate him even more.

"Shut up, you bitch! You encouraged this! You probably pushed her to dishonour her father once again!"

"Dad, she had nothing to do with this. Stop yelling at her."

"Do not lie to me, Tamara! Do not become like her!" he boomed standing up. "I will not allow you to become a slut like her! And you are still seeing the same boy. Like your mother, you are a deceiver." He grabbed my arms and pulled me towards him. His eyes were ablaze with disgust.

"Joseph, please don't start!"

"Is Charlie home?" He spat the question at her.

"I don't think so, Joseph," my mum replied, sighing.

"Tamara, I will not allow your mother to corrupt you. You are my daughter. I work hard only for you, so you can make me proud. I educate you and give you everything you need so you can have the future I never had."

"Dad, I know. You tell us that all the time. We appreciate it, really we do, but—"

"Let me finish!" he hollered, and I instantly lowered my eyes and flinched, afraid he was going to slap me again.

"I work like a dog so you can have a good life! Your mother disappointed me long ago, and I will not allow you to continue doing the same. You must know the truth." I wished he would just talk in English and get to the point. The look on my mother's face was scaring the shit out of me, and my arms were aching. I wanted to tell him to let me go but didn't dare.

"Joseph, I want to tell her!"

"You have no such right! You slut! You are the cause of my heartache."

"Joseph! Please, stop now. It wasn't like that; I want to explain, and you never allowed me to. You never wanted to talk about it. Let me explain before you tell her, please."

"No! What can you possibly say to change things? You were the one who cheated! Tamara, Charlie is not my son. I refuse for you to turn out a slut like your mother!" He paused, and I tried to make sense of what he had just said. "Your mother had an affair, and Charlie is not mine. He belongs to that bastard, Andre!"

"Mum, what? Is this true … is what he is saying true?"

"Yes," she replied with tears flowing down her face.

"Tamara, I became a hard father because of your mother. I didn't want you to be like her."

"Please, Tamara. Let me explain," my mother began.

"Explain what? That you are the cheater! Mum, how could you do this? All this time, I thought Dad was the tyrant, the one who didn't know how to love, but how could he after you were unfaithful to him?" I knew my words were breaking her heart, but I couldn't stop. My fury was just as brutal as my father's. "You were the unfaithful one! All this time I thought he was definitely the cheater, but it was you! Oh my God! How could you do this? How could you do this to us? How could you damage this family even more?"

"I …" my mother's sobs took control, and she couldn't continue her sentence.

"You were always my ray of light, Mum; you kept me sane all these years. But now I hate you both. I always thought I was the illegitimate one. I always prayed and hoped I was adopted or that I wasn't his, yours!" I cried looking at him. "I always told myself not to be stupid, though, that you couldn't possibly be like that, Mum! I feel like I don't know anything anymore! But one thing I do know for certain is that I don't belong here! I don't belong in this fucked-up family! I am better than all of you!" I spat the words at both of them, my eyes darting from her face to his.

"Tamara, please," my mother said. Her eyes changed as she looked behind me. I turned and saw Charlie standing in the doorway.

"How could you do this, Mum?" Charlie asked, his face as red as my dad's.

"My children, please understand that it wasn't just me. He …" she began pointing her finger towards my dad.

"Do not dare blame me for this," my father roared as his hand came up and slapped my mum across her already bruised cheek.

"Don't fucking hit her," my brother roared as he grabbed my father by the collar and raised his fist.

"Go ahead, hit the only father you have ever known," my father stated in a steely voice.

"Hitting a woman is wrong!" Charlie said.

"Go ahead and be a French pussy. See if I care; you are not my son," my father replied much to all our astonishment. Charlie's eyes became small slits, and he pulled his arm back. He then sighed and lowered his fist.

"See, you are a pussy. Your cousins would be real men, and they would hit me," my dad muttered. Charlie walked away from him and punched the wall on his way out. The plaster dropped to the floor in pieces, and as I stared at the broken pieces, I knew our family had fallen apart, as well. I ran after Charlie, but he was already cycling down the street too quickly for me to catch up to him. I rushed back into the house, grabbed my bag, and bolted back outside. I ran all the way to the train station and headed to my auntie's. I called Sara, and through my sobs told her, that I'd be at her place soon.

There were a few people giving me funny looks on the train, but I didn't care. I couldn't stop my tears from streaming down my face. I was crying for myself, as well as Charlie. God knew what he must be feeling! But I was wondering why it wasn't me? Why wasn't I the illegitimate one? I was and forever will be related to that tyrant. His temper and his family's inherent jealousy and cruelty will always flow through my veins. I wished more than anything that we had never found out! This changed everything. When it rained drama in my family, it fucking flooded!

I stared at the picture of Adrian and me on my phone and wondered how he would react when he found out about all this. His family would forbid him to continue seeing me. Adultery in a wog family was even worse than abuse. They would never look at me or my mother in the same way. His father would tell him to stay away: After all, like mother, like daughter, right?

As soon as Sara opened the door, I rushed into her arms and couldn't stop crying long enough to explain what had happened. She held me and let me cry out all my anger and despair. Her mum came home, held me by the arms, looked me straight in the eyes, demanded I stop crying and explain what happened. After I breathed in my last shaky breaths, I told her everything.

"*Khalto*, I didn't mean it! I was just so shocked, so angry! As his words tore at my heart, my words broke hers. I could see it in her face," I whispered as the tears began to flood my eyes again.

"It's OK, Tamara. She will forgive you. Mothers forgive their children everything. But now we have Charlie to deal with."

"Yeah, we have to go get him, but first I need to talk to Mum." My auntie just nodded and picked up the phone.

CHAPTER 16

When Mum walked into the living room, I stood up slowly.

"Mum, you know I didn't mean it. Any of it," I muttered, finally meeting her eyes.

"I know, *habibti*," she replied and held out her arms to me. I walked towards her and hugged her tightly. We pulled away, and I wiped her tears away.

"Sit down; let's talk. Tamara; I need to explain."

"You don't have to, Mum."

"Yes, I do, and I need to tell Charlie, too," she paused and looked over at my aunt who nodded encouragingly. "You need to know why."

"From what you told me this morning, I understand, Mum. Dad shouldn't have let his family tear you two apart. How can I blame you for looking for love elsewhere if you didn't get it at home?"

"Yes, true, and it was also my mother's death. When you were just two months old, I went to my mother's funeral in Lebanon. I tell you before what a shock it is for me, her dying of cancer and me not with her, instead half way other side of world. All day, I cry for her and me. I hated your father then, Tamara, hated his family, and hated him more and more because he let them treat me bad. He became bad, too, and working all time, and he ignored me. I felt lost and no one love me. He hit me when I told him I wanted to stay longer than for funeral. He said you can't leave me to cook and clean for myself! You can't leave me looking after Tamara. He did not tell me that he understood that your mother died and you need time. He was cold, and I could not remember man I had married. I missed you and didn't want to leave you, and I love you, but you were little, just a baby. I could not get much love from you. Your father show you all his love and me nothing. I know, stupid that I was jealous, but I felt too alone. Anyway, I see Andre at my mother's funeral. After he come to the house and I leave, I need to get away from all the people. He follow me with his car. I get in, and he drive me to Beirut. We have coffee at restaurant and talk and talk. He still not married; he tells me he still love me. I start crying, and we walk back to his car. He hold me so tight, and I let him. I tell him everything I feel. The first few weeks I stay in Lebanon, he come to see me all the time. Nelly, my little sister, did not think right, and her husband, too, but they not say anything. They know I not happy with your father."

"But Mum, didn't other people see you?"

"Yes, they did and they talk. Your father calls and tells me I have to come home now. I was not allowed to stay, and he needed me, and you needed me. He did not ask about Andre, but I heard his voice. He was afraid and supic … suspic."

"Suspicious, Mum."

"Yes, suspicious. I told him I will look if there is early flight. I found one after a week. I told Andre, and he asked me to stay. To stay with him. But I wouldn't leave you, Tamara. I could have left your father, but not you. On the last night, Andre cooked for me at his house, and we make love. I know then that I loved him, always did, but was stupid little girl when I meet him. I still love him now, and I still don't know if I love your father. Tamara, we share a child together, but I have been ignored all the time from your father. When I come home after a month, I see I'm pregnant, and your father and I never, well, when I return. He suspicious, and he never touch me. He know not his, and I tell him about me and Andre. He beat me, and then as my stomach grow, I beat myself and try to lose it, but your brother too strong. He came, and your father did not divorce me, but we become more strangers. He wants you to have a mother, so I stay. I never told Andre about Charlie, and I never go back to Lebanon.'

"Fucking hell, Mum. That's epic!"

"Language, Tamara!" she said sternly.

"Sorry, but why, Mum? Why haven't you returned? Your sisters want to see you and meet us. They always tell me over the phone to convince you and dad to go."

"Tamara, if I see Andre again, I go crazy. I never go back," she replied looking down at a photo. She reached over and handed it to me. I glanced down at a picture of a very good-looking man with startling green eyes, framed by very long black eyelashes.

"He is so handsome, Mum."

"He still is. I saw him last year," my auntie stated.

"What?" my mother replied, bewildered.

"I didn't tell you because I knew it would upset you. He still is good-looking," my auntie said with a smirk. "You should go see him. You owe that to Charlie."

"I don't know. Tamara, you forgive me? I am sorry for being human."

"It's OK, Mum. It's alright really," I replied, handing back the photo and holding her hand. "Mum, I think you really need to go to Lebanon."

"You think so, too?"

"Yes. Firstly, we need to find Charlie, and you need to explain this to him, and I'm pretty sure he will want to meet his father."

"Joseph will never allow that," my mum stated.

"Too bad!"

"Tamara!"

"What, Mum? Things have to change, and we can no longer pretend to be a happy family when we're not. Now that your secret is out, we have to be honest about everything."

"Life not that easy, Tamara."

"I know, Mum, but all we can do is try. Do you really believe that Dad will divorce you?"

"Yes, and he will keep you, not Charlie. Why would I do this?"

"Why do you have to keep living this miserable life?"

"It is a sacrifice all mother willing to make if she love her children."

"Well, I think it is time we sacrifice a bit for you, Mum," I replied, putting my arms around her. She stiffened and then relaxed, squeezing me tightly. God knows how long Mum hadn't had any physical affection for. I knew now why our family was always uncomfortable to show affection in any way.

"I … Tamara *habibti* …"

"You don't have to say anything else, Mum. I will talk to Charlie; he'll be at Amelia's. *Khalto* will you drive me over there. Mum, you stay here; I'll get him to come over here, OK?"

"OK," she replied, smiling at me warmly. I saw so much pride and love reflected in her eyes, and I hoped that one day I would be as amazing a person as my mother was.

As we got into the car, I looked over at my auntie and knew she wanted to say something. "What? Come on, *khalto*. Spill."

"I'm glad you are the person you are, Tamara *habibi*."

"Thanks, I think, but I really don't see what the big deal is."

"You realise that right now, you are being the adult. You are the one who is trying to fix this situation."

"Yeah, I guess I am. I hope Charlie listens, though. I'm afraid he will never forgive her."

"I'm sure he will," my auntie answered.

CHAPTER 17

As soon as we arrived at Amelia's house, I tried to call Charlie, but his phone was off. When Amelia answered the door, she took one look at me, turned around, and shut the door. I turned to walk back to the car, but stopped when I heard the door latch.

"What do you want?" Amelia asked me with a sigh.

"Is Charlie here?"

"Maybe," she replied stepping outside and leaving the door slightly ajar.

"Amelia, I'm really sorry for ratting you two out," I muttered, stepping towards her.

"Whatevs …"

"Seriously, if I could take it back, I would. I was just so angry at Charlie for ratting *me* out, and my temper got the better of me. Are you OK? I mean after the …"

"After what? After your dad forced us to kill our baby? How would you be?"

"Oh God, I'm so sorry," I replied holding my arms out.

"What? You think you are going to hug me? Like one hug will forgive everything! Your father won't even acknowledge me, Tamara!"

"He won't acknowledge Adrian, either."

"But I was pregnant with his grandson!"

"It was a boy?"

"Yeah," she sighed again and sat on the porch steps. I sat beside her, and we both stared straight ahead.

"I wish I could take it back."

"Your dad would have found out either way. Charlie wanted to get rid of it anyway. Fuck, we're only fifteen! He just didn't have the money and then when your dad gave it to him, well …"

"Your parents are cool, though. They let Charlie come over all the time. I thought they would have, you know, supported you keeping it."

"My parents are cool, but not about me having a kid at fifteen. They want me to become something, and a kid would stop that from happening. Plus, Maltese parents aren't that different from Lebo ones. They don't want people talking and calling me a slut and stuff. Lucky, I don't have any brothers, or Charlie would be dead right now," she told me with a sad smile.

"You really love him, yeah?"

"Yeah, we're gonna get married when we're eighteen and have as many kids as we can afford." I laughed with her. I hoped my future sister-in-law and I would become close friends one day.

"Is Charlie OK?"

"Not really. It took him a good hour to finally tell me what was wrong. I'll go get him. You guys really need to talk," she said as she stood up. I followed her lead.

"Thanks, Amelia," I replied as I leaned over and hugged her. She hugged me back, cleared her throat, and walked inside.

"Hey," Charlie muttered as he walked outside.

"Hey, bro," I replied wanting to reach out and give a hug. "Can we talk for a bit?"

"Yeah, sure." We sat down on the front steps, and I wondered what the best way to start this conversation was.

"So how fucked up can our family get, eh?" he stated with a smirk. I laughed with relief and put my arm around his shoulder.

"How badly do you hate us all right now?"

"I hate Mum more than anyone," he sighed and continued, "and I hate dad, too, but I couldn't even hit him!"

"That's because you are a better man than he is."

"All this wouldn't have happened if it wasn't for Mum!"

"She wants to explain, Charlie; you got to hear her side of the story."

"Whatever she says won't make things different."

"That's what I thought, too, but once I heard her side, I understood."

"Understood what? Why she is a lying cheating …" I was glad he stopped himself.

"Charlie, she had her reasons. Please come over to *khaltos*; she is waiting in the car."

"Mum is?" he replied startled.

"No, *khalto*," I replied placing my hand on top of his. "Please say you will."

"All these years, I thought Dad hated me cause you were so good, and I was a troublemaker," he paused and looked away. "I hated how he loved you more," he continued, "I hated you, blamed you! That's why I told dad about your lies and everything else. I'm sorry, Tam."

"It's OK. I'm sorry for snitching on you, too," I replied hugging him. "Dad loves you, Charlie, but you just remind him of what she did to him."

"I'm not even his son; he doesn't give a flying fuck about me and never will. You heard what he said before!"

"Charlie, please don't say shit like that. He does love you, trust me. And so does Mum."

"Whatevs …" he got up and headed back inside.

"Charlie, please give Mum a chance to explain. Please, let's try to mend this fucked-up situation."

"Why the fuck should I?"

"Cause I know you love Mum, and you don't want her to suffer any more than I do. We both hate seeing her so miserable, and I know you don't want to add to that misery."

"But it is her fucking fault, Tam!"

"No, you will see that they are both at fault, as well as Dad's family ... please just listen to her." He looked past me for a long moment; I could see the tears welling in his eyes, and just like Mum, he was able to make them disappear. He nodded and followed me to the car.

As soon as we walked into *khalto's* living room, Mum stood up, put out her cigarette, and just stared at Charlie. He stared back, and the tension in the room was suffocating. Mum looked at the carpet and then raised her eyes up to Charlie's as the tears began to pour down her face.

"I am sorry, *habibi*. I am sorry, I am sorry." She choked back her sobs, and I glanced over at Charlie as he was trying to swallow his. She moved towards him and touched his shoulder. He turned and hugged her while she stroked his hair. *Khalto* and I left them to be alone. I walked up to Sara's room and knocked on the door.

"Come in," she yelled.

"Hey, cuz," I muttered as I sat on her bed.

"Hey, Tam. How you doing?" she asked as she typed away at her computer.

"Hoping all goes well with Charlie and Mum."

"Me, too," she replied as she said bye to Shadi and signed off Facebook.

"How's Shadi doing?" I asked her as she sat beside me.

"Yeah, he is good," she replied with a smile, "he finally told me he loved me last night."

"Really? That's awesome, babe," I squealed as I gave her a big hug.

"You know, when I first dated Shadi, I was so afraid he was going to be a typical Lebo and be all jealous and crazy like my dad was. But he really surprised me. He is so open-minded, Tam, and so down to earth about everything."

"When I talked to Charlie before, I realised he didn't rat me out cause he was an arrogant, macho, overprotective Lebo. He did it because he was jealous of how I was Dad's favourite. He never understood why, and I never saw it. I never thought that I was treated better because he got away with everything. I saw today how badly he felt being the dud of the family while I was the star."

"It's hard to be compared to you, Tam. You are too intelligent for your own good and too mature sometimes. Even my mum compares me to you sometimes," she informed me dryly.

"Shit, Sara. I didn't know that. Sorry."

"It's cool; it's not your fault. You can't help who you are. But let *us* enjoy the limelight sometimes, OK?"

"OK," I stated throwing the pillow at her. "Sara, do you miss your dad?"

"Sometimes," she looked away and didn't meet my eyes, "but then I remember what a prick he was to mum and me and then I wonder how could I miss that."

"Yeah …" I didn't know how else to respond.

"But he is still my dad, and if he wanted to see me one day, I wouldn't say no. I don't think I will."

"So if he sent you a plane ticket to go Leboland, you would go?"

"Yeah, probs … But not for long. I would miss Shadi too much."

"What about your mum and me?" I sulked.

"Yeah, maybe just the tiniest bit," she replied, punching me playfully on the shoulder. I walked with her downstairs, and we sat in the kitchen, anxiously waiting for Mum and Charlie to walk out of the living room. When they finally did, both smiling, Charlie playfully punched me on the shoulder, and I pinched his cheek before he slapped my hand away.

"All OK, my Tamara. All OK," my mother whispered in my ear as she hugged me.

"Charlie, mum needs to go to Lebanon and you need to meet your biological father," I said to both of them.

"Yeah, I want to meet him mum," Charlie agreed.

"I think you should go to Lebanon tomorrow mum." I told her seeing the fear in her eyes.

"What! No, I can't. Too soon, I need to speak to your father," Mum replied.

"Don't worry, we will talk to Dad."

"Are you sure Tamara?"

"Yes mum, we are sure. Right Charlie?"

"For sure!" He replied hugging Mum tightly.

At that moment, my phone rang and Fiona's name flashed on the screen.

"Hey, bimbs. What's up?"

"Tam, hun, are you sitting down? Maybe you should sit down."

"Come on, Fi, stop being silly. What's wrong?"

"Tam, don't freak, but Rania Saab died last night."

"What! How?" I asked as I slumped down on a chair nearby as Sara looked at me quizzically.

"She overdosed on eckys. She mixed eckys with those major pain killers they gave her after the abortion, and her heart stopped. Fuck, her mum is hysterical."

"Who told you all this?"

"From her brother Anthony. He goes to school with my little bro, remember? And they are good friends. He is over at our place right now; he couldn't stand being at the hospital with all his relatives pretending they care. He lost it at his dad and blamed him for her death. It's bad shit!"

"Oh my God," I muttered.

"Weren't you with her last night?"

"What?"

"Yeah, we were chatting on Facebook, and you said you were going with her to Wissam's party and that she was fun and me and Mi Mi weren't."

"Ah, Fi, yeah … we will talk about it tomorrow."

"Rania's funeral is tomorrow. They want to have it over and done with. Anthony goes, it's like they want to forget about her as soon as she's buried. Poor kid!"

"Alright, Fi. Thanks for letting me know. I'll see you at the funeral tomorrow then."

"You OK?"

"Yeah, kind of. You?"

"Yeah, kind of, too."

"Alright, bye, babe." I hung up the phone and repeated what Fi had told me.

"Fuck! You're shitting me!"

"Sara! Language!" My aunt yelled.

"Sorry, Mum, but oh my God! This shit just doesn't happen!"

"Yeah, it does," I replied, "and I never helped her or talked to her cause she was such a bitch to me. Now I realise she was more messed up than I could have ever imagined." I let the tears roll down my cheeks as my mum held me in her arms.

"We better go home and I need to pack before your father come home. Time to think of me." I smiled and nodded in agreement and followed my mum out the door. I turned and saw Charlie hovering in the doorway.

"I think I'll stay here tonight if that's OK, *khalto*."

"Of course, *habibi*," Auntie Lydia replied.

"'I'll come to the funeral with *khalto* tomorrow," Charlie said as Mum hugged him and told him she loved him.

Dad wasn't home when we arrived, and we went to sleep wondering if he was coming home at all. I couldn't fall asleep. Why was *she* dead of all people? Not that I wished it upon anyone else, but Rania had gone through so much for someone so young. Sara texted me asking me what had happened at the party. I replied that I couldn't remember a thing cause I got so drunk and that we would talk about it tomorrow. I couldn't deal with all the questions. *Was I responsible? That's the last thing I want to think about now. But you will have to eventually. I know! Just shut up for now!*

I got up and turned on my computer at about two in the morning. I started writing in my diary — well, typing. I noted the events of the day and how I was feeling. I still couldn't believe that she had died. I started thinking about how I would feel if a member of my family died. I thought that a big part of me would wither away, too. Mr Saab and Mrs Saab's only daughter had just died. I shook my head and knew that Rania would never intentionally take her own life. I reckon if she had wanted to, she would have done it straight after the abortion.

I decided I would rather be a school counsellor than a psychologist. At least I could prevent kids from taking drugs and accidently overdosing. My whole outlook on life had changed the moment I heard Fiona tell me that Rania had died. What is it they say? When a life ends, you see yours in a whole different light. I think I read that somewhere. Well, mine was looking different alright, but I couldn't quite say if it was in a positive or negative light at that moment.

CHAPTER 18

THE NEXT MORNING, MUM AND I were both relieved when we saw Dad emerging from the guest room. We all got ready for the funeral in silence. No one spoke a word, and Dad left before us. I was apprehensive about the funeral, as I had never attended one before, and I was dreading the inevitable conversation I had to have with my dad. How could we move forward from here? Would Dad kick Mum out now that we knew her secret? Would he hire the best lawyer possible and fight to have full custody of me? I changed my outfit a few times, unsure of what was appropriate for a funeral. I had never been this indecisive before.

When Mum and I reached the church, we found Charlie, *khalto*, and Sara waiting for us out the front.

"Did you see Dad?" I asked Charlie.

"Not yet," he replied, shrugging his shoulder as if he couldn't care less when we both knew he was freaking out. We walked in together and sat behind Dad and Rania's family. I had forgotten Dad and Rania's father were friends. During the whole service, I kept glancing at the back of Dad's head. I wondered what he was thinking and what he was going through. Not once did he turn around to glance over at us.

Halfway through the service, Dad got up to say a prayer of the faithful. He glanced at the floor as he walked up to the altar. As he read his prayer, he did not look up once. He looked dazed and confused. He was not my father today. He was not the arrogant, self-assured man I had always known him to be.

I started crying towards the end of the ceremony and couldn't go up to view the body. I wondered how a service was being conducted considering there was a possibility she had killed herself, but then again, no one really knew if she had meant to overdose or not. I bet all Rania wanted to do was scare her dad a little so he would pay attention to her again, so he would show her love instead of anger and disgust.

After the service, everybody went to the cemetery. I looked around at everyone dressed in black, surrounding the coffin. They looked like withered flowers swaying in the wind, their heads bowed like petals before they fall off the stalks. I saw Adrian and his dad to my left. I wondered why they were there, and Mr Fontana walked up to Rania's dad and shook his hand. I hadn't realised they were acquainted. I stood to the side and texted Adrian. He came over after he read my text, and we hid behind a tree. I made sure no one was looking before I hugged him.

"You OK?" he asked me stroking my cheek.

"Not really, you?"

"I didn't really know her, but Anthony goes to my school. He's a good kid."

"She wasn't bad. Just troubled, particularly after the abortion," I replied with a distressed sigh.

"I love how you always see good in people, not that I'm saying she was bad, but she was mean to you, yet here you are defending her."

"If only you knew what she went through, Age, you would do the same."

"I don't want to keep all this from you anymore, Age. I think I am responsible for Rania's death."

"Tam, don't be ridiculous! Why would you think that?"

"Cause I was with her. I took an Ecky with her. Maybe if I didn't go that night, she wouldn't have overdosed," I stated as the tears blurred my vision.

"Tam, you can't force anyone to take drugs," he replied, taking my hand in his.

"Yeah, I know, but I was with her in the bathroom. I freaked out and left her there! Do you understand what I am telling you, Age?" I yelled through my sobs. "I fucking left her!"

"Shhh," he whispered in my ear as he hugged me. He stroked my hair until I stopped crying.

"You were scared; I get that."

"I was a fucking coward!"

"But it isn't your fault. Like you said she was troubled, and she drowned her sorrows in alcohol and drugs."

"Maybe I could have stopped her," I whispered in his ear. He pulled back and looked deep into my eyes.

"No, you couldn't have! Now stop blaming yourself, OK?"

"It is easier said than done," I sniffled and hugged him towards me. I knew this feeling of guilt would linger for a while, but how could I not blame myself? Every time I closed my eyes, I saw Rania lying on that bathroom floor. I didn't think I could ever truly forgive myself for running away and leaving her there.

"You didn't end up telling me what happened when you got home yesterday," he said as he pulled away and held my hand.

"It's too long of a story to talk about now, but Age, would your parents make you stop seeing me if my parents got a divorce?"

"What? Are they going to?" he asked startled, looking at me with deep concern.

"They might, long story short, my parents have never really had a good relationship. Dad and his family treated Mum really badly. Mum went to Lebanon when her mother died and bumped into an old love interest and realised she had loved him all along. Charlie's not my dad's son."

"Fuck! That's major news. Is he OK? Your mum? When did this all go down?"

"Yesterday. I'm glad everything is out in the open, but I don't know where we're going from here. Mum is going to Lebanon tonight. Your parents will definitely forbid you from being with me if they ever found out about Mum's infidelity, won't they?"

"Stop worrying about my parents. No one will ever keep me from seeing you, I thought I had proven that to you already," he said as he ran his fingers through my hair. I smiled up at him and hugged him again. I whispered goodbye and walked back to where my mum was standing. Before we left, we walked over and expressed our condolences to Rania's family. Dad was standing next to the family, and we had to kiss him too, even though he was a part of our family and not hers (weird Lebanese funeral traditions). I saw him and my mother embrace and thought I saw tears floating in his eyes, but when I came to kiss him on the cheek, he seemed fine. I walked back towards Rania's dad as he was talking to the priest.

"Mr Saab, I just wanted to say," I paused not knowing how to continue, "I don't think Rania wanted to harm herself. I think she was just scared and disappointed with herself."

"Thank you, Tamara, I appreciate this. But I would always tell Rania to be more like you, a good girl like you, but she would not listen. Now she is gone." He turned away and wiped at the corner of his eye. I realised then why she hated me. She kept messing up, and she hated that her dad was always angry with her and always comparing her to me. I walked away as quickly as I could and cried all the way home. If only he knew the truth about me. What would he do if he found out I was with her that night?

CHAPTER 19

Dad finally arrived home at about nine and found Charlie and I watching television in the living room.

"Where is your mother?"

"She's at the airport, she is leaving for Lebanon tonight."

"What?!" He seemed angry but mostly broken.

"Dad, we need to talk about yesterday." I said, getting up and sitting on the chair beside him.

"What is there to say?"

"Well, it's about time we are all honest with one another, Dad. Now that the truth has come out, we need to discuss where we're going from here."

"We are not going anywhere; we are staying the same as usual. Your mother will be back, she always comes back home."

"Not this time Dad," Charlie finally piped up. "Mum is miserable, and you blame her for everything when it is your fault, too."

"Of course you would defend her!"

"Both of us are defending her; don't think that because Charlie isn't your son he doesn't care about you. He does! But Dad, you pushed her away. You pushed her into Andre's arms, and it was partly your fault and partly your family's fault."

"Your mother is a cheater!"

"Dad, don't get angry at me for being honest with you," I said.

"Yeah, Dad, I mean, shit, you're still my dad to me," Charlie added, and my father just looked from him to me.

"You kids are so grown up. Now you will leave me, too, and I will have no one."

"Don't be silly, *baba*; you will always have us, and we are family. Charlie is going to go to Lebanon as soon as the holidays start. I think he needs to meet his biological father."

"And you?" Dad asked, looking at me with the saddest eyes.

"I'll follow them later. I want to meet him too."

"Will you return?"

"Of course, Dad; my life is here."

"So is mine," Charlie stated. 'I will never live in Lebanon. It is not my country or my home. And I can't leave Amelia. I love her."

I looked over at Dad and saw how broken he was. It had finally dawned on him that he had lost Mum. My heart hurt for him but I also couldn't help but wonder whether Mum would get together with Andre. What would happen? Would she stay there or bring him here? Would my parents get a divorce and get us for half the time each? Where would I want to live if I had the choice? I started hyperventilating thinking about it all and then I told myself to calm down. Whatever happened in the future, we would deal with as a family.

"Everyone will wonder why your mother is in Lebanon all of a sudden. The suspicions my family have will be proven right."

"I'm sorry, Dad but we can't keep living our lives worrying about what your family think!' Charlie almost shouted.

"Dad, it will all be OK," I told him as I placed my hand over his. "At least we're all honest with each other now. Don't be hard on yourself; you couldn't have prevented this if you had tried."

"When did you become so wise?"

"I guess I take after both my parents," I replied with a smile.

"Charlie, you know you are always welcome here. This is still your house, and I still consider you my son. I would always threaten to only take Tamara with me, but that was because I wanted to hurt your mother as much as she had hurt me." He cleared his throat and looked down at the floor. "I do love you both," he stated looking at Charlie and then me. I leaned over and gave my dad a hug. He then stood up, walked towards Charlie, hugged him, and patted him awkwardly on the back. We all sat down and watched the Arabic news. Charlie and I knew it wouldn't be right to leave dad alone right now.

That night, after dad went to bed, I checked my emails and found one from Miss Mitchell, asking me to say a few words at Rania's memorial service at school the next day. I sighed and hated the burden placed on me. Then I remembered Rania's eyes and how sad they were after she was forced to abort her child. I instantly felt guilty and replied to Miss Mitchell that I would be honoured to speak at the service. I also knew I owed Rania this; I was with her before she died, I felt obliged.

I stared at the blank computer screen for a long time. I finally started typing, and the words flowed easily. I just hoped that Rania's father was not going to lunge towards me and try to kill me after I had finished what was needed to be said.

CHAPTER 20

As I walked up the aisle at the chapel, I kept telling myself to breathe and stay calm. I was so nervous that I still felt like I wanted to throw up. I had tried to for half an hour, my head over the toilet seat, but I couldn't make myself do it. I hadn't eaten anything all morning, my stomach was growling, and my mouth was dry. As I took my first step up the altar, I lost my footing and landed on my left knee. The sound echoed through the chapel, and I felt my face flush red. I stood up, continued up the stairs, and finally turned around. I almost laughed out loud. My eyes skimmed all the people in front of me until I saw Mariam and Fiona smiling encouragingly towards me. They had been so supportive this morning, and it made me love and appreciate them even more. They instantly forgave my crazy behaviour when I told them about being with Rania that night. They understood that I was trying to figure out who I was and instantly reassured me that I hadn't contributed in any way to her death. I glanced down at Rania's father and gulped down my anxiety; I couldn't back out now.

"Good morning, family and friends of Rania Saab. When Miss Mitchell asked me to make this speech, I was terrified. What could I possibly say to honour Rania in the way she deserved to be honoured and remembered? She was a valued student, friend, sister, and daughter," I paused and smiled sadly at Mr Saab, "and she will be missed by all the girls in year ten. To be completely honest, Rania and I were never close friends. I think Miss Mitchell chose me to speak because I am head of the debating team and because I had known Rania since we were both in nappies." I stopped and scanned the crowd.

"But I don't think that is the reason I am up here today. I need to speak for Rania, because it could easily be Rania up here talking about me. I could have gone down the same path that she chose. Rania and I have always had this competitiveness, always wanting to outshine each other somehow. Rania was so beautiful, the tallest in our year level, and the first to have a boyfriend." I heard Rania's father clear his throat, but I continued, "Rania and Wissam were so in love with one another, and all us girls envied her. After everything she went through and…" I made the mistake of looking over at Miss Mitchell who was signalling for me to stop right there. I ignored her and the stricken look on Mr Saab's face and continued, "Um, well, something in her died. Parents sometimes do things they think is best for everyone, but really, it is only best for them, even though they do it out of love. They truly believe it is in our best interest, but parents can be as misguided as we teenagers are the majority of the time." I looked down at my hands and blanked out. What was I meant to say next? Fuck!

"Rania changed after she lost um after everything she lost, and I wish somehow I had done something to help her get back on track. Love is a great thing and shouldn't be condemned. Rania's memory will always live on, and I have learned one thing from her death. Caging someone will only cause harm. Even if that imprisonment is out of love and concern." I finally lifted my eyes and breathed in deeply. "Parents should help their children find the strength to amend their mistakes. Rania, we all wish you were with us, and you were loved by so many people here, including me, although I never realised it till now." I took a deep breath and willed myself not to cry in front of all these people. I avoided eye contact with everybody and basically sprinted down the aisle. As soon as I was out of the chapel, I heard someone call my name and I quickened my pace.

"Tam, hold up!" Finally, I realised it was Adrian's voice, and I swiftly turned around. He bolted towards me and hugged me tightly. I finally allowed myself to cry.

"What are you doing here?" I asked him as I pulled away from his warm embrace.

"As if I wouldn't be here for you. I've been trying to get in contact with you all morning. Why didn't you reply?"

"I forgot my phone at home, but I'm so glad you're here," I replied with a hug.

"That was quite a speech," he said, wiping my tears away.

"I think I overdid it. I just kind of rambled on towards the end, and my emotions got the better of me."

"I love your passion, and I love you, Tamara Khoury." I stared at him and saw that love emanating from his eyes. I kissed him passionately but couldn't say anything back. He stroked my hair as if he understood why I was silent as I leaned my head on his shoulder. I pulled away from him as Mariam and Fiona walked towards us.

"Tam, that was admirable. So proud of you, babe," Mariam stated as she hugged me.

"Me, too," Fiona added as she hugged us both. I clung to both of them and was so thankful for them and the greatest, most loving boyfriend a girl could ever wish for. I felt guilty knowing Rania should have had that, too, but knew those guilty feelings would soon subside.

Dad and Charlie joined us and hugged me in turn. My father was about to say something, but Mr Saab was walking towards us. I couldn't look at him. I was terrified of what he was going to say and even more what he was going to do! All I could picture was him storming towards me and slapping me and then demanding to know how I had the audacity to speak about his daughter that way. I mean, my father would do the same thing. My heart was beating so loudly, and I felt like I was going to pass out! I realised I had been holding my breath the whole time. I began to tremble as he got closer. I managed to look up and meet his eyes. "Mr Saab, I'm sorry if that."

"Tamara, wait," he interrupted. "Do not apologise." He paused and stared intently into my eyes. I began to hyperventilate and thought he must hate me so much. I had never been so terrified before, and I waited in agony for the slap or the humiliation or the reprimand.

"Thank you," he simply stated and walked off towards where his family was waiting.

"I have never been so proud of you, Tamara," my father informed me.

"Same here," Charlie added.

"You must be, Adrian," my father said to Adrian as he held his hand out.

"Yes, sir. Nice to finally meet you," Adrian replied, shaking his hand firmly.

"You will come over for dinner tomorrow, OK?"

"Yes, sir, that would be an honour." I tried not to laugh out loud as Adrian stammered and smiled awkwardly at my father. I could not believe this was happening. Any minute, I expected myself to wake up. But this wasn't a fantasy. It was actually happening, and I couldn't be happier. My family members said their goodbyes and walked away.

"I'll be right back, guys," I told Adrian, Fiona, and Mariam.

"Dad," I began as I walked towards him. "Thanks for inviting Adrian over. You don't know how much that means to me."

"Tamara, what you said before is true. Parents shouldn't try to control their children in every way. I am sorry I was so hard on you about that boy, but he seems like a good young man. As long as he keeps treating you with respect, he is welcome in my house," my dad replied with a smile.

"Thanks again, baba," I said as I leaned over and hugged him. He cleared his throat and walked over to where Charlie was standing. I headed back and leapt into Adrian's arms and kissed him.

"Wow, you're coming to dinner," I squealed in his ear as he grimaced.

"Uh huh, can't wait for more awkwardness," he replied with a cheeky smile.

"Right! Off to class, Tamara, Mariam, and Fiona," we heard Miss Mitchell say as she clicked towards us in her heels.

"Bye, Age," I whispered into his ear as I embraced him one more time.

"Bye," he called out as he walked away. I turned to walk to class and noticed Wissam walking towards me.

"Hey Tamara," he said as he looked down at his shoes.

"Hey, Wissam," I replied, also avoiding eye contact.

"Why did you just bolt of the party like that?" he asked with a frown.

"What?"

'You didn't even wait for the ambulance. How could you just leave a friend like that?" He asked with frustration and anger as he curled up his fists.

"Wissam, please try to understand. I was terrified."

"Bullshit! You are a fucking coward! You shouldn't have been given the right to speak up there," he almost yelled turning away from me.

"Wissam, wait," I began as he slowly turned around. "I feel terrible as it is! Nothing you can say will make me beat myself up more than I already have. I am a fucking coward, but I made that speech to show Rania I am sorry. I know it isn't enough, but I will keep trying. I will be a better person than I was that night, and maybe one day, even if it's years from now, I will be forgiven for deserting her."

He sighed with sadness.

"I am going to talk to her every day and hope she hears me," I stated, sniffling and wiping my tears away.

"Alright, Tamara. It's OK."

"You know what? It really isn't. I will never forgive myself for leaving her. I am a coward and chicken shit and wish I could take it all back." I turned away from him and grabbed another tissue from my bag. I felt his hand on my shoulder, and I turned around.

"Really, Tamara, stop. It is OK. She would have really appreciated what you said in there."

"Thanks, Wissam, for being nice. I don't deserve it!"

"No worries," he replied and leaned over and hugged me. "Your words about Rania were true."

"Thanks," I said as I pulled away. "Are you gonna be OK?"

"Yeah, I just miss her, regret so much …" I tried not to look at his eyes as they were filling up with tears.

"She loved you, you know."

"Yeah, I know," he punched me affectionately on the shoulder. "You are a good person, Tam. Even though you are crazy sometimes, ultimately, you have a good heart," he said as he tucked a strand of my hair behind my ear. I smiled up at him, tears forming in my eyes once again.

"You don't have to say that."

"I never say things I don't mean," he replied as he leaned over and kissed me on the cheek and walked away. He turned back and smiled back at me with the sweetest and saddest smile. There was also something else in his expression that I just couldn't define. I smiled back, and as soon as he turned away again, I placed my hand on my cheek.

CPSIA information can be obtained
at www.ICGtesting.com
Printed in the USA
BVHW032139101019
560840BV00001B/41/P